J series

Also by L. Divine

THE FIGHT

SECOND CHANCE

JAYD'S LEGACY

FRENEMIES

LADY J

COURTIN' JAYD

HUSTLIN'

KEEP IT MOVIN'

HOLIDAZE

CULTURE CLASH

Published by Kensington Publishing Corporation

Drama High, Vol. 11

COLD AS ICE

L. Divine

Dafina KTeen Books
KENSINGTON PUBLISHING CORP.
http://www.kensingtonbooks.com

DAFINA KTEEN BOOKS are published by

Kensington Publishing Corp.
119 West 40th Street
New York, NY 10018

All Kensington titles, imprints, and distributed lines are available at special quantity discounts for bulk purchases for sales promotion, premiums, fund-raising, educational, or institutional use.

Special book excerpts or customized printings can also be created to fit specific needs. For details, write or phone the office of the Kensington Special Sales Manager: Kensington Publishing Corp., 119 West 40th Street, New York, NY 10018. Attn. Special Sales Department. Phone: 1-800-221-2647.

KTeen Reg. U.S. Pat. & TM Off.
Sunburst logo Reg. U.S. Pat. & TM Off.

ISBN-13: 978-0-7582-3113-0
ISBN-10: 0-7582-3113-X

First Kensington Trade Paperback Printing: June 2010

10 9 8 7 6 5

Printed in the United States of America

This book is dedicated to my mother, Dorothy Lynnette,
the strongest woman I know.
I pray that I always live up to your reflection.

ACKNOWLEDGMENTS

"I can't base what I'm gonna be off of what everybody isn't."

—JAY-Z

I would like to say thank you to all the visionaries who have triumphed over the inevitable challenges present on this journey by sharing their talents through their art. The world can be a cold place, no doubt. I grew up believing that—for the most part—life was about suffering, that the world was not a safe, secure place, and that joy existed only on television. I have since learned that, yes, that is definitely one view of this multifaceted life, but there is also the balance. Move through the suffering to get to the joy, and never limit your vision based off what other people tell you is possible. They may not see what you see so easily when it first becomes apparent to you, but they will have no choice but to acknowledge your vision once it becomes too real to ignore. Only you can dream your dreams, and, therefore, only you can make them reality. Don't just dream it, live it, and the world will become a warmer place because of it.

THE CREW

Jayd

A sassy sixteen-year-old from Compton, California, who comes from a long line of Louisiana conjure women. She is the only one in her lineage born with brown eyes and a caul. Her grandmother appropriately named her "Jayd," which is also the name her grandmother took on in her days as a voodoo queen in New Orleans. She lives with her grandparents, four uncles, and her cousin Jay. Jayd is in all AP classes and visits her mother on the weekend. She has a tense relationship with her father, whom she sees occasionally, and has never-ending drama in her life, whether at school or home.

Mama/Lynn Mae

When Jayd gets in over her head, her grandmother, Mama, is always there to help her. A full-time conjure woman with magical green eyes and a long list of both clients and haters, Mama also serves as Jayd's teacher, confidante, and protector.

Mom/Lynn Marie

At thirty-something years old, Lynn Marie would never be mistaken for a mother of a teenager. Jayd's mom is definitely all that and with her green eyes, she keeps the men guessing. Able to talk to Jayd telepathically, Lynn Marie is always there when Jayd needs her.

Netta

The owner of Netta's Never Nappy Beauty Shop, Netta is Mama's best friend, business partner, and godsister in their religion. She also serves as a godmother to Jayd, who works part-time at Netta's Shop.

Esmeralda

Mama's nemesis and Jayd's nightmare, this next-door neighbor is anything but friendly. She relocated to Compton from Louisiana around the same time Mama did and has been a thorn in Mama's side ever since. She continuously causes trouble for Mama and Jayd. Esmeralda's cold blue eyes have powers of their own, although not nearly as powerful as Mama's.

Rah

Rah is Jayd's first love from junior high school, who has come back into her life when a mutual friend, Nigel, transfers from Rah's high school (Westingle) to South Bay. He knows everything about her and is her spiritual confidant. Rah lives in Los Angeles but grew up with his grandparents in Compton like Jayd. He loves Jayd fiercely but has a girlfriend who refuses to go away (Trish) and a baby-mama (Sandy). Rah is a hustler by necessity and a music producer by talent. He takes care of his younger brother, Kamal, and holds the house down while his dad is locked up and his mother strips at a local club.

Misty

The word "frenemies" was coined for this former best friend of Jayd's. Misty has made it her mission to sabotage Jayd any way she can. Living around the corner from Jayd, she has the unique advantage of being an original hater from the neighborhood and at school.

KJ

He's the most popular basketball player on campus, Jayd's ex-boyfriend, and Misty's current boyfriend. Ever since he and Jayd broke up, he's made it his personal mission to persecute her.

Nellie

One of Jayd's best friends, Nellie is the prissy princess of the crew. She is also dating Chance, even though it's Nigel she's really feeling. Nellie made history at South Bay by becoming the first Black Homecoming princess and has let the crown go to her head.

Mickey

The gangster girl of Jayd's small crew, she and Nellie are best friends but often at odds with each other, mostly because Nellie secretly wishes she could be more like Mickey. A true hood girl, she loves being from Compton, and her man with no name is a true gangster. Mickey and Nigel have quickly become South Bay High's newest couple.

Jeremy

A first for Jayd, Jeremy is her white ex-boyfriend who also happens to be the most popular cat at South Bay. Rich, tall, and extremely handsome, Jeremy's witty personality and good conversation keep Jayd on her toes and give Rah a run for his money—literally.

Mickey's Man

Never using his name, Mickey's original boyfriend is a troublemaker and always hot on Mickey's trail. Always in and out of jail, Mickey's man is notorious in her hood for being a coldhearted gangster, and loves to be in control. He also has a thing for Jayd, but Jayd can't stand to be anywhere near him.

Nigel

The new quarterback on the block, Nigel is a friend of Jayd's from junior high and also Rah's best friend, making Jayd's

world even smaller at South Bay High. Nigel is the star football player and dumped his ex-girlfriend at Westingle (Tasha)
to be with his new baby-mama-to-be, Mickey. Jayd is caught
up in the mix as a friend to them both, but her loyalty lies
with Nigel because she's known him longer and he's always
had her back.

Chance
The rich, white hip-hop kid of the crew, Chance is Jayd's drama
homie and Nellie's boyfriend, if you let him tell it. He used to
have a crush on Jayd and now has turned his attention to
Nellie.

Bryan
The youngest of Mama's children and Jayd's favorite uncle,
Bryan is a dj by night and works at the local grocery store
during the day. He's also an acquaintance of both Rah and KJ
from playing ball around the hood. Bryan often gives Jayd
helpful advice about her problems with boys and hating girls
alike. Out of all of Jayd's uncles, Bryan gives her grandparents
the least amount of trouble.

Jay
Jay is more like an older brother to Jayd than her cousin. Like
Jayd, he lives with Mama but his mother (Mama's youngest
daughter) left him when he was a baby and never returned.
He doesn't know his father and attends Compton High. He
and Jayd often cook together and help Mama around the
house.

Prologue

The tickle down the right side of my neck distracts me from keeping up with the steady pace of Jeremy's lips. He started out kissing my left ear and then moved on to my right. Now Jeremy's focus has returned to my mouth, and I'm glad for it. I love the way his soft lips feel against mine even though him kissing my neck is definitely my next favorite thing. I could lie on this couch with him forever as long as he keeps making me feel this good.

Jeremy and I have been making out for what seems like hours, but I'm not worried about the time. My phone's gone off twice since he got here, and I couldn't care less. I know it's Rah ready to grill me about seeing Jeremy kiss me on Friday night at the race, but I have nothing to say to him about what we do. I just hope we don't stop anytime soon. The second time around for Jeremy and me just might be what we both need.

"I'll give you a thousand dollars for that thought," Jeremy says, pulling away from my lips and promptly kissing me on my nose. We both need to come up for air, but not for too long, I hope. It's been a while since I had a make-out session without having to look over my shoulder for a crazy ex-girlfriend or baby-mama on attack mode.

"And you probably would, too," I say, kissing Jeremy on his neck. By the way he's shaking, I can tell he likes it. I keep kissing, softly biting his flesh as I smile at every involuntary jump he makes.

"Come on, Jayd. I'm serious," Jeremy says, kissing me on my right cheek and then again on my ear. If he doesn't stop, we're going to get into some serious trouble I know I'm not ready for. I'll be seventeen in a couple weeks, and all my friends are waiting on me to lose my virginity because I'm the last one in our crew and probably the whole damn school. But I'm not going out like that—not yet. Jeremy continues, "From now on we need to have full disclosure—no secrets. That's the only way this can work."

"Full disclosure? I'm not sure I can do that," I say, easing my way out from under him and sitting up straight on the small couch that doubles as my weekend bed at my mother's apartment. The couch was already a mess before Jeremy got here, and now it looks like a tornado hit it. The pillows are strewn across the living room floor, with my sheets and blanket across the coffee table. If my mom walked in right now she'd be more upset by the mess in her apartment than the boy making out with her daughter.

"Why not?" Jeremy asks in that innocent way of his that makes my heart melt. He's so adorable when he's on a mission for information. "Look, Jayd, I'm serious about having a committed relationship with you, and that means we have to be completely honest with each other, even if it means having to hear something we might not want to. So what's on your mind?"

I look into Jeremy's blue eyes and see his sincerity. But I still don't feel comfortable telling him everything about how I, Mama, and my mom get down.

"Because, Jeremy, there are some things I can never tell

you or anyone else about my life," I say as Jeremy sits up next to me. "It's not that I don't want to tell you or that I'm keeping anything from you on purpose. It's just the way it is. I hope you can understand." I really, really do. Me being a voodoo priestess is a big adjustment for Jeremy, I know. But it's a nonnegotiable part of my life that all my friends have learned to deal with in one way or another.

"I can respect that, Lady J. I can't help but hope that one day you can tell me everything, no holds barred." Jeremy pulls me into his arms, and I accept his warm embrace. He always smells fresh, like Irish Spring and seawater. It must be from all the surfing he does on a daily basis. "Anyway, I have to get going. I'm meeting the gang at the pier and still need to get my boards from my bro," he says, kissing me on the back of my neck before letting me go.

"Not yet," I say, rising with him. "We've got all day." I know I have a ton of things to do before I head back to my grandmother's house in Compton this evening, but all that can wait if he'll stay.

"Ah, baby, I wish I could stay and hang, but we have a surf competition coming up, and we're in need of some serious practice." I never knew surfing was more than a hobby to Jeremy. I had no idea he competed outside of his crew, just like I didn't know that he and Chance drag raced for money. It seems like I have a lot to learn about my elusive friend.

"Full disclosure, huh? You have a few secrets of your own I'm not privy to, don't you, Mr. Weiner?" I ask, pushing him on his lower back as we walk to the front door. He's got a cute butt for a white boy, and I love his strong, tan legs, even if they are covered in hair.

"We all do. But for you, Miss Jackson, I'll be an open book." Jeremy turns around and strokes my face with the back of his right hand before bending down for one last kiss. I gently grab the back of his head, entangling my fingers in his thick curls. Jeremy's hands move from my face down to my waist, and he pulls me in closer. Here we go again.

"Damn. Do you have to go now?" I whine as he releases me from his embrace. Jeremy opens the door and steps over the threshold, officially ending our make-up make-out afternoon. Every time Jeremy kisses me like this, I feel swept away in the moment. This fool's got some power over me, and we both know it.

"I love you, too, Jayd," Jeremy says, kissing me on the forehead before jogging down the stairs without allowing me to respond. That fool just said he loved me and ran off. What the hell?

I step back inside and close the door as my phone rings once again. I push the silence button and notice the time, realizing I need to get a move on, too. I just remembered I was supposed to meet my crew at Nigel's house about an hour ago. No wonder Rah's been texting and calling me like crazy. I lost complete track of time, but that's how it is once Jeremy and I get started, and I don't regret a single minute.

While relocking the multiple bolts on my mom's front door, I swear I can feel someone's eyes on me. I walk over to the living room window and look outside over the neighbor's tall trees to see if I notice anyone staring my way. I don't have time to play 007 right now. I have to clean up this place and get ready to go, which includes a shower and doing my hair. It's still early in the afternoon, and I know my crew's not going anywhere anytime soon. I'll be there as soon as I can, but I'm not rushing for anyone. Besides, I feel too good from Jeremy's surprise visit and love confession to care about being late or who may be spying on us. I just want to enjoy this feeling a little while longer before I have to deal with my crew and their inevitable issues.

~ 1 ~
The Ultimate Betrayal

*"Yuh need fi check yuhself before yuh start kiss yuh teeth /
Caw yuh nuh ready fi this yet, bwoy."*

—TANYA STEPHENS

Once all my chores were done at my mom's apartment, I gave my hair a quick wash and dry before flatironing it and packing my stuff. It's been a minute since I've had time to give my hair the proper love and care it deserves, but hopefully next weekend I'll have more time to pamper myself. I sent Mickey a text a few minutes ago, informing her I was on my way. I don't even know why I'm going to this session. I have schoolwork to catch up on, and there are always Mama's assignments to do. Will a sistah ever get a break?

When I pull up to Nigel's house in Lafayette Square, a stone's throw away from Crenshaw Blvd, I see all my friends are in attendance this sunny Sunday afternoon. I wish I were at the beach with Jeremy, as nice as the weather is. I park my mom's little gray ride behind Chance's Chevy and turn off the engine. Maybe I can take Chance's car around the block before we leave. I need to make it a habit to drive his and Jeremy's cars more often so I can sharpen my hot-rod driving skills. I wonder if girls ever race in their car crew?

"Sorry I'm late, y'all. What did I miss?" I ask, entering Nigel's foyer and greeting my friends chilling in the living room. They all look distracted by whatever's on the flat-screen television. I'm surprised Nigel's girlfriend, Mickey, would come back so soon after Mrs. Esop called her out last week about being unsure of the paternity of her unborn child. But I guess my girl's still hopeful she'll be accepted into the family. If there is ever an eternal optimist in the darkest of challenges, it's Mickey. She's dead set on marrying Nigel and becoming a housewife, even if his mama can't stand her.

"Damn, Jayd. You missed everything. Nellie and I are almost done with the registry and guest list," Mickey says, flipping through baby catalogs, which has been her and Nellie's favorite pastime lately. I'll be so glad when this baby is born, I don't know what to do. I walk into the living room and join the session in progress. I know they didn't smoke down here, but my boys are definitely floating high on cloud nine.

"You must've been real busy to be almost three hours late. Where were you?" Nellie asks, tagging several pages with pink Post-it notes. Party planning is definitely my girl's thing. Maybe she can plan a small birthday celebration for me this year. My birthdays are usually uneventful, but I wouldn't mind doing a little something on my special day. Nigel and Chance nod their greetings without looking away from the Chow Yun-Fat flick in front of them. Martial arts always mesmerizes my boys, and he is one of my favorite actors, too. Looks like I came just in time, no matter what Nellie and Mickey may think.

"She was with her boy toy," Rah says, taking his red eyes away from the fight scene on the big screen to glare at me. I knew he would be irritated about seeing Jeremy kiss me on Friday, but he really can't say shit. I have to endure not one but two of Rah's ex-heffas sniffing around him on the regular. Jeremy and I actually have a future together, unlike Rah and me.

"He's not my boy toy," I say, ready to defend Jeremy and me if need be. "I know you know me better than that, Rah." I roll my eyes at him and sit next to Nellie on the couch. Mickey and Nigel are cuddled up together on the love seat, and

Chance is sitting on the floor in front of Nellie while she plays with his hair. Everyone's coupled off except for me and Rah, yet we're the two who brought them all together. Isn't this ironic?

"Then what is he, Jayd?" Rah asks, turning his body to face me completely. "You're usually not late to a session, and you didn't answer my calls or texts. Naturally, I got worried and went by to check on you. Before I could get out of the car, I saw your boy, Jeremy, leaving your mom's apartment, and he looked very happy," Rah says, waiting for my confession, but from where I'm sitting I don't owe him an explanation.

"Oooo, a midafternoon make-out session. I love it," Nellie says, taking her hands out of Chance's head and clapping. "Details, please." Nellie is a bit too excited for the heaviness of the situation between me and Rah. I'll fill her in on the encounter, kiss by kiss, another time. Right now I need to check my boy before he goes too far.

"Rah, Jeremy and I are friends, and you've known that all along. Besides, you don't see me spying on your ass when you don't answer my calls, which is quite often now that Sandy's back in your life," I say, sucking my teeth at him. He's got nerve enough for the both of us, with the way he carries on with his daughter's mother.

"Jayd, you can say whatever you like, but you know you're wrong to be dealing with that punk again. He shouldn't even be touching you," Rah says, his high cheekbones flexing at the very thought of Jeremy and me kissing. I didn't mean for him to ever witness Jeremy and me being affectionate, but it happened and there's no going back.

"Hey, that punk is my friend, and he helped you win that basketball game against KJ, don't forget," Chance says, having Jeremy's back like a true homie. Nigel has Jeremy's back, too, but he's Rah's homie first, so he's silent, for the time being. But I know if Rah gets too carried away, Nigel will step in. We all know Rah's not really pissed at Jeremy; he's just jealous because I'm doing my own thing.

"Whatever, man," Rah says, calming down for the time being, or so I think. After a few minutes of silence, Rah comes back at me. Am I going to get to watch the movie in peace or what?

"Just admit that the shit was disrespectful, Jayd, and I'll let it go." Mickey and Nellie look at Rah and then back at me. Nigel feels the gravity of the situation and turns the volume down on the surround-sound system his dad hooked up in here. The entertainment system in the game room is even tighter than this one, and I already feel like I'm at one of Magic Johnson's theaters. But Rah's drama is distracting us all from watching the movie.

"I'm not admitting a damn thing," I say, now just as irritated as Rah. This fool is really tripping and messing up my vibe. I was feeling good when I left my mom's house, especially after Jeremy told me he loved me. Now I feel like kicking Rah's ass. "Can you please shut up so we can enjoy the movie? We'll talk about it later." If I were a dude, Rah would've socked me in my mouth for telling him to be quiet. He looks like he's going to hit something, and I feel him.

"You've lost your damn mind, you know that?" Rah says, standing up from his seat and towering over me. "Do you really think I'm stupid, Jayd? I know you and that punk-ass white boy are more than friends—no offense, man," Rah says to Chance, who looks like he wants to jump in but chooses against it. When Rah gets this angry, there's no reasoning with him. Nigel gets up from his cozy spot next to Mickey just in case he needs to cool Rah down.

"Come on, man. Let's take a walk," Nigel says, trying to distract him. But Rah's eyes are set on me, and mine on him. Nellie scoots over, putting more space between her leg and mine. Chance scoots over on the floor just in case Rah takes another step and accidentally crushes Chance's fingers under-neath his new Jordans.

"You betrayed me, Jayd. You betrayed us," Rah says be-tween his teeth before storming out of the living room and through the front door, passing Mr. and Mrs. Esop on his way down the porch steps. Nigel looks down at me and shrugs his shoulders before following his boy. I haven't seen Rah this angry with me in a long time.

"Rah, wait a minute. It's not that serious," I say, rising to follow them out. He can be so dramatic sometimes.

"Hello, Jayd," Mrs. Esop says, leading her husband through the open door. I smile at Nigel's mom and dad before walking through the foyer. They look stunning in their Sunday best, fresh from church.

"What's wrong with Rah?" Mr. Esop asks, turning his head to watch Rah start his car while Nigel tries to reason with him. Then Mr. Esop heads to the game room next to the living room. Mrs. Esop takes off her large white hat and smoothes down her hair while looking in the antique mirror hanging in the entryway.

"Oh, the usual," I say, looking back at my crew, who are looking at us instead of the muted screen in front of them. A live show is always more interesting. "I'll be right back," I say, adjusting my purse on my shoulder and walking down the steps. I'm so sick of doing damage control, but it's an un-avoidable part of maintaining friendships. And sometimes boys can be more difficult to deal with than girls when it comes to matters of the heart.

"Jayd, I'm looking forward to continuing our discussion about you becoming a debutante soon," Mrs. Esop says. I thought I was out of that deal when she went off on Mickey the other day.

"But I just assumed you wouldn't be interested in coming to the shower anymore," I say, trying to speak low so Mickey doesn't hear. I haven't told Mickey about my deal with Mrs. Esop yet. But from the look on her crooked face, I'd say Mickey has heard the entire conversation. Shit. Now I'll have to deal with her drama, too.

"Just because it's not my grandchild doesn't mean I can't enjoy the festivities," she says with a cunning smile. "And I am nothing if not a woman of my word. Besides, a deal's a deal," Mrs. Esop says, waving to Mickey, Nellie, and Chance before walking up the stairs. Mickey looks at me like she's going to explode, she's so pissed, but I'll have to deal with her later. Why does my life have to include all this bull? Right now I have to catch Rah before he does something stupid, which is the usual when his head gets this hot.

"Yes, ma'am," I say, making my way out the front door. I guess I'll have to catch up with Rah later because he's already gone, and I'm in no mood to pick out baby clothes or to be grilled by Mickey. All that will have to wait until tomorrow. I just want to live a little longer in the moment Jeremy and I had earlier. I should've stayed right where we were—damn reality. But, in reality, shit happens, and my friends always seem to be in the thick of it.

Whether it's the weekend or a school day, there's never a boring moment in my life. Luckily, I had plenty of school and spirit work to distract me from yesterday's argument with Rah and impending debate with Mickey. So far it's been a relatively quiet morning. I made it through Spanish and English class without running into Misty or Mickey. It's a shame that one of my best homegirls gives me the same feeling of dread as does my worst enemy, but only when Mickey's in rare form like I'm sure she is today. Mickey's had all night to think about it, and, hopefully, she came up with the reasonable solution—that I, as her friend, would never do anything to intentionally hurt her. But judging by the way she's storming down the main hall, I'd say she's thinking just the opposite.

"So when were you going to tell me you were trying to get in good with Mrs. Esop for your own benefit?" Mickey says, fronting me at my locker like she's going to beat my ass. What the hell? Chance and Nellie are right behind her.

"Mickey, I don't know what you're talking about," I say, opening the long metal door and almost hitting her in the face. She'd better back up before I lose my patience. Rah's been working my nerves since last night, and I'm in no mood for any more drama, hormonally driven or otherwise.

"You know exactly what I'm talking about. You're using my baby shower to get closer to Nigel's mama so you can join her little sorority and be all uppity and shit," she says, rubbing her bulging belly like it's a golden crown. I'll be so glad when she finally has that baby, I don't know what to do.

"That's some cold shit right there, Mickey," I say, looking at my girl in disbelief. How could she think I would do something like that to her? I never wanted to be a debutante, let alone one involved with Nigel's mom. She has to know I would never betray her trust, and for what, a night as the black Cinderella? Please. I'm not Nellie. This shit is right up her alley. I half wish Nellie had been asked instead of me, but I already know Nellie doesn't have the grades to participate. Otherwise, I'm sure she would jump at the chance to be in a cotillion.

"Okay, ladies. Let's take a step back for a min," Chance says, trying to lighten the mood, but it's no use. Mickey's gone off the deep end and is determined to take everyone with her.

"Take a step back for what? So Jayd can twist the knife she planted in my back a little deeper? I don't think so, white boy," Mickey says, drawing more attention from the majority of white students walking through the hall on their way to class—which is also what we should be doing. Mickey's already on academic probation for ditching school on the regular. The last thing she needs is another incident on her record.

"Okay, there's no need to go off on my man, Mickey," Nellie says, stepping between us. "He's just trying to help."

Mickey looks from Nellie to me and then back at Nellie. I hope she doesn't think Nellie's taking sides, because we're all in this together whether Mickey likes it or not.

"Mickey, let's take a walk," Nigel says, taking his girl's right hand and attempting to lead her away, but she's not budging, no matter how wrong she is right now.

"Not until Jayd admits she was in the wrong for accepting your mom's invitation when she knew it belonged to me." Even Nigel has to smile at his girl's twisted logic.

"Mickey, you can't be serious," I say, shaking my head at my girl's overactive imagination. She can blame it on pregnancy all she wants, but I know better. This girl's just straight tripping off some jealousy bull, and I'm not hearing it, especially after all I've done for her lately.

"I am serious, Jayd. This is my family, not yours, so butt out."

Without saying a word, I slam my locker door shut, zip up my backpack, and throw it over my shoulder. I then look my livid girl dead in her eyes, thinking of a way to respond without making her cry, but thankfully Nigel steps in.

"Babe, Jayd's not trying to take anything from you. The truth is, my mom asked her because she's known Jayd for years and respects her stride. It has nothing to do with you."

"The hell it doesn't," Mickey says. "And whose side are you on anyway, Nigel?"

"Mickey, you make everything so damned difficult," I say. I'm trying to spare my girl's feelings, but it's not worth it. "Nigel's mom said if I participate in the ball, she'll come to

your shower. That's why I'm doing this—for you, not me."
The bell for third period rings in the now still air, causing
everyone around us to stir, but we remain at a standstill. For
a moment I think Mickey's coming to her senses, but then
she opens her mouth.

"Whatever, Jayd. You can't stand the fact that you're not
the only girl in your little boy crew anymore, and I'm not
falling for it." This girl needs to get over herself, but that'll
never happen. Mickey's nothing if not the truth about her
shit. "You can go ahead and have your little ball, but I've got
the real deal right here, and you can't take this away from us.
Rah's right: You're nothing but a traitor." And with that final
verbal blow, Mickey holds on to her baby bump and struts
down the hall. That girl is unbelievable.

"Jayd, I'll talk to you later," Nigel says, following Mickey
out of the building. Chance and Nellie head out, too, after
apologizing for the stupid scene. It's cool—I'm not going to
let Mickey get to me, especially when I know how ignorant
her ass is going to feel once she realizes how wrong she is.
There's nothing I can do about it now, and we all need to get
on with our day.

Unfortunately it's already been a long week and it's only
Monday. Not only is Mickey tripping way too hard for me to
deal with—and also try to help her pregnant ass at the same
time—but Mrs. Bennett dropped a bomb of her own today,
announcing that the mandatory Tuesday and Thursday AP
meetings were over. Instead, we will have practice AP exams
twice a week until the actual exams a few weeks from now. A
bitch is a bitch and then some. At least Mickey left a half-
assed apology on my voice mail for going off on me earlier,
but it wasn't that genuine, in my opinion, and was probably
prompted by Nigel, I'm sure. I didn't make a big deal out of
it, but as far as I'm concerned, she still owes me a real one.

When I made it home this evening, the house was quiet. I didn't check the spirit room to see if Mama was here, because, honestly, I just wanted a moment to myself before everyone else got home. With my four uncles, grandparents, and cousin Jay all living under one roof, it gets pretty crowded around here. It's days like this that I miss the weekends I spend at my mom's apartment.

"How was your weekend, baby?" Mama asks, coming through the kitchen door from the backhouse in which the spirit room is housed. I jump up from my seat at the kitchen table to help her with her bags of dried herbs and other spirit tools. It looks like she's about to make a spiritual bath. I hope it's for her own use because she looks more tired than usual. Her green eyes look weary, and her shoulder-length salt-and-pepper hair is pulled back in a bun—the usual style when she doesn't feel like bothering with her hair.

"It was okay," I say, retrieving the bags and closing the back door behind her. "How was yours?"

"Busy, girl," she says, making her way back to her bedroom, and I dutifully follow. "We have an initiation to assist in, starting at the end of the month, Jayd." Spring and summer are the seasons Mama's called on by other spiritual houses to help with their new initiates, as well as any other rituals that may come up. Mama gets hella cash for participating in ceremonies, even though she never asks for a dime. Sometimes she works for free, saying that her payment will come from Legba, which it always does in one way or another.

"You know, my birthday's also at the end of this month," I say, reminding her even though I know it's not necessary. I place the items on Mama's bed and follow her back into the kitchen. I guess there's more where that came from.

"So is your mother's, but neither one of the days are holidays, and we still have work to do," Mama says, stepping out the back door. That's the same thing I told Mickey's unborn child when I walked through Mickey's dream last month. Nickey Shantae is more like me—her spiritual godmother—than I thought. No wonder she chose me to protect her little spirit self.

"Okay, okay," I say, packing up my schoolwork spread across the kitchen table and putting it in my backpack on the floor. I can see Mama will need this space. Mama steps back inside with a covered serving plate and sets it on the kitchen counter. She opens the top, and I can smell the raw chicken from here.

"Did I miss something?" I ask, watching Mama wash her hands and then the carcass in the sink. During certain ceremonies, preparing chicken is a mandatory sacrifice.

"Yes. Netta's son received Shango this weekend," Mama says. "We finished his ritual earlier this afternoon, leaving us with dinner." People often forget where fried chicken comes from, with a Popeyes on every corner, but Mama prefers it the old-fashioned way. "And do you know somebody around here had the nerve to call Animal Patrol on us because we had live chickens in the backyard?" Mama places the whole bird on the cutting board next to the sink and chops it into separate parts before placing it back on the plate to marinate.

"What did you tell them?" Voodoo practitioners have always come under attack by animal-rights folks or unsympathetic neighbors. I take out the sea salt, pepper, and other seasonings and place them on the counter.

"I told them the truth. We don't have to hide anymore," Mama says, seasoning the poultry. She'll fry part of it and bake the rest. "But you still didn't tell me how your weekend really was. Did you get any work done?" She expertly flips the meat, evenly coating every piece. Damn, that's going to be good.

"Yes, but not too much. There was drama with Rah to distract me, as usual," I say, walking to the dated stove and turn-

ing the dial to heat the oven. Mama washes her hands and
moves on to the herbs on the kitchen table as I remove the
two large cast-iron skillets and place them on the stovetop.
This stove is on its last leg, which is why I'm saving up for a
new one on Mother's Day.

"How's that beautiful little girl of his?" Mama asks while
separating the various plants—some for dinner, some for the
bath. How she remembers what goes where is amazing to
me.

"She's okay, except she still has a crazy mother. I had to
pick up Rahima from Sandy's job one night because of Sandy
and her games," I say, washing my hands in the sink before
moving on to my next task. I love being in the kitchen with
Mama.

"Sandy's job?" Mama asks, almost dropping some of the
rosemary stems on the kitchen floor, which needs mopping
badly. That's my uncles' job, but they rarely do their fair share
of chores around here. "Doesn't she work at a strip club?"

"Yes, she does," I say, recalling the less than favorable memory in my head while taking the large bottle of olive oil from
the kitchen cabinet and pouring it into the skillets for the
fried chicken. "How she could take her baby there is beyond
me, but who am I to judge?"

"You are a child of Oshune. That's who you are to judge,"
Mama says, looking at me and scrutinizing my thoughts with
her eyes.

We finish up the preliminary cooking duties now, ready to
get down, which means I need to change clothes. Battering
chicken is a messy job, and my Apple Bottoms top is too cute
for that.

"We don't do that, Jayd." Mama takes the herbs in our
bedroom to dry, and I follow with my backpack and purse in
hand.

"Do what?" I ask. I close the door, take a seat at the foot of my bed, and kick off my sandals before changing clothes.

"Participate in deviant behavior. And taking a child to a seedy place like that is definitely abnormal." Mama places the herbs with the other things on her bed and lays them all out to get a better look at her collection. After I finish dressing, she takes out a few of them and hands them to me to inhale.

"I know it was a bad judgment call, but I couldn't leave Rahima there. And I told Rah and Sandy that it wasn't a good idea, but they just thought I was making a big deal out of nothing."

"There is so much power in being a woman. If that girl only knew," Mama says. "Put those in your bath tonight and sleep in clean whites to remove some of that negative residue you've got lingering on you from your friends. Some people will never learn that all money ain't good money."

I hear that loud and clear. Unfortunately, much like Mickey, all Sandy cares about is getting a man to pay her bills, and Rah's the lucky guy. She'll have as many babies as it takes to secure her future. Whatever happened to working for yours? It's just like choosing to cook dinner or buy it—either way, there's work involved, but in the end, what you put in is definitely what you get out. And both Mickey and Sandy are in for a rude awakening with the choices they're making. It'll be a cold day in hell before I sell myself out like that.

~ 2 ~
Cold As Ice

"It's a cool world, and I'm destined for greatness."

—MIKE JONES, FEATURING NICOLE WRAY

*T*he *room is dark except for a flicker of light coming from a lit candle sitting nearby on an antique writing desk. There's also a feather pen and ink chamber on the desk and a blank writing pad. I walk toward the desk, curious about the ancient writing tools, but I hesitate before I claim them with my hand. I can feel Mama's presence behind me, gently pushing me forward.*

"Go ahead, dear. Write it down. It's your story to tell," Mama says to me, guiding me to sit in the leather chair behind the desk. But how can I write in the dark?

"Mama, I can barely see. Can I get some light in here?" I look around the dark room for a window, lamp, something that will give me a little more brightness, but no such luck. The candle is the only assistance I have, and it's not very bright.

"You have all the light you need, chile. Now go on and get busy. We don't have all night."

I take my seat at the desk and begin writing as much as I can, but I can barely see the words forming on the white page in front of me. I dip the pen into the black liquid and pray that what I'm writing is legible. I know what I want to say, which is half the battle. But whoever reads it may not get the full meaning of my words if they can't make out my handwriting. I was never good at penmanship.

"Why am I writing this down when no one's going to be able to make it out? Isn't that the point of keeping up with our history?" I ask Mama, who has since disappeared from the room. I take a deep breath and continue my scribing, more anxious to get on with this assignment so that I can leave this dark space. It's giving me the creeps.

Finished with my story for the moment, I rise from the weathered seat and walk toward the only opening in the dark space. As I reach for the barely visible brass knob and open the door, I feel a cold breeze enter the room, giving me the chills. I take a step outside, momentarily blinded by the bright light coming in from every direction, and immediately fall flat on my ass, hitting my head on the cold, hard ground.

"Damnit! What the hell was that?" I ask aloud, holding the back of my head where the pain throbs. I'm not sure who's listening, but I can feel someone's presence around me.

"Watch your language, young lady, even when your head hurts," Mama says, gently scolding me, but I know she can feel me. That shit hurt. "And that was black ice, Jayd. It's the most dangerous kind because you can't see it until it's too late. Always watch your step, even in the light," Mama says, but I can't see her. All I see are the stars in my head, like in a cartoon.

"Ouch," I say, slapping the alarm clock and rubbing the back of my head where the impact from the fall in my dream has left a knot in reality. Why can't I dream like a normal person?

"Because you're not normal, Jayd," Mama mumbles from her side of the room. "Now go on and get up before you're late. And put some ice on your head. It'll help the swelling go down," she says, turning back over to return to her slumber. Isn't it ironic that the same thing that hurt me is the same thing that'll help me heal? I wish I could stay under the warm covers, but I have to get up and start my day—weird dream, knotted head, and all.

It's a beautiful spring morning, not that we in California know much about the seasons changing at all. But I can feel the sun's warmth breaking through the foggy ocean chill on my skin, and I welcome the constantly hot days that are ahead. Let's just hope that nothing at school will ruin my mood. So far, so good. It's already lunchtime, and no one's pissed me off as of yet. But it's still early in the day, and I have an African Student Union meeting plus two more classes to get through before I can officially declare this day drama free. But Nellie and Mickey are getting me closer to pissed with this constant baby-shower planning, especially since Mickey has yet to officially apologize for her rude behavior. I could give a damn about what she's going through, being on academic probation, pregnant, or whatever. Mickey accusing me of betraying her ass was cold-blooded and can't be easily forgotten or forgiven.

"Okay, it looks like the shower will have to be the weekend of the twentieth because the following weekend is Easter and we all need to be in church that Sunday and shopping for our outfits the day before." Nellie and her parents go to church only on the major holidays, paying their tithes and sporting their designer fashions for all to envy. Isn't that breaking one of the Ten Commandments—thou shalt not make people covet your shit?

So far we are the only ones present for the ASU lunch meeting, which is why Nellie's taking over as the official shower dictator. I thought we were planning this together, but I guess I thought wrong.

"Um, but that's when I want to celebrate my birthday," I

say. I would add that I don't celebrate Easter, but that's irrelevant right now. It's a shame that I have to remind these heffas of my birthday when they expect everyone to stop traffic for their special days. Maybe if I had a little more bitch in me like my girls, they'd remember.

"Oh, Jayd, now, that's just selfish," Mickey says. "The baby precedes everything else." I know this heffa's not talking about me being selfish. Didn't we all just duck and dive bullet shots because of her necessity to cheat on her boyfriend, a notorious gangster?

"Excuse me for not wanting to talk about someone else's party on my birthday weekend," I say, looking around Mr. Adewale's classroom as students file in for the lunch meeting; I am tired of my self-centered friends. "I don't mean to be a diva, but damn. When is it ever about me in this crew?"

"Yeah, Jayd. This is so unlike you," Nellie says. I know she's not serious. "We have to make sure the baby gets everything she needs." She flips through the catalogs on her desk like she's getting paid to do this party.

"Yes, when she gets here. We still have a couple months before that happens. My birthday is one day, this day, and I want to celebrate it. I turn seventeen only once," I say, snacking on the last of my pretzels before moving on to my cranberry juice. They were all out of my favorites at the lunch counter today, so I had to switch it up.

"Oh, speaking of birthdays, can you come with me tomorrow evening to Chance's house? His mother's having a little dinner celebration for his father's birthday, and I need backup. It's my first time meeting his parents, and I want to make a good impression." Did Nellie hear a word I just said? Speaking of selfish. If there were a crown for the most selfish broad alive, Nellie would have that title, and Mickey would be first runner-up.

"Nellie, I don't think so. I've got a lot of studying to do," I say, officially pissed. "On top of my regular schoolwork, I have the AP exams coming up soon, and I really need to be on top of my game." I've been so distracted with all my friends' and family's bull that I've been neglecting my own responsibilities, and that's not a good thing, because I clearly see that my friends don't have a sistah's back like I always have theirs.

"Okay, everyone, how are we doing this afternoon?" Mr. A asks, entering the classroom with a large manila envelope and a smile. He makes my day. "Ready to nominate a treasurer to hold the African Student Union's precious money?"

"Hey, Mr. Adewale," Misty says, strolling into the lunch meeting like she's not late. Mr. A announced at the last meeting that people who are late will not be allowed to vote on the day's issues, and if they continue to be late, they'll be eliminated from votes and field trips for the entire semester. He doesn't play with time, and time is money, so I completely understand.

"Miss Caldwell, you are five minutes late, which means you forfeit today's votes," Mr. A says, tossing the envelope on his desk and taking a seat in the chair behind it. Misty sits down in her seat next to KJ, for whom she had brought lunch. That's probably why she's late. When will she learn that dudes never respect doormats?

"Oh, come on, Mr. Adewale. I didn't know the lunch line was going to be so long. The cafeteria helpers really need to speed things up. It's not my fault they were slow today," Misty says, taking one of KJ's fries off his tray, not realizing how serious Mr. A is about his shit.

"A lack of planning on your part doesn't constitute an emergency on mine," Mr. A says to a salty Misty. That's one of his favorite sayings, and he uses it daily, much to many students' disliking. "Now, we have several officer positions that need to be filled before we can move on as a group. Secretary, president, vice president, and treasurer are all up for grabs. We should start with the money because we have an envelope full that needs to be taken care of as soon as possible," he says, gesturing to the envelope on the top of his stack of papers. And I thought I had a lot of work to do. "Any nominations for treasurer?"

"I think it should be me. I love holding paper," KJ says, his crew dutifully laughing. He can barely keep up with his own wallet, let alone the African Student Union's bank account.

"Yes, baby, and you're good at it, too," Misty says, forever his cheerleader. My ex–best friend and ex-boyfriend make the perfect stupid couple, and because of that, they are the last two people in this club who should be taken seriously.

"Oh no. We need someone responsible, and we all know that ain't you," I say, causing others in the room to snicker through bites of their lunch.

"What are you talking about? I'm very responsible," KJ says, pleading his case. "Have you seen me take the ball up the court? You can always trust me to do my job." He seems sincere, but even he can't be that clueless. Nothing about KJ screams treasurer.

"Does Trecee ring a bell?" I ask. KJ had unprotected sex with her, and she was nothing close to clean. If that's not being irresponsible, I don't know what is. I hope Misty's being smarter about using protection than he's known to be. "If we can't trust you with your own body, we sure as hell can't trust you with our money."

"That was cold, Jayd," Del says, shaking his head at my low blow. Before KJ can respond with his visibly steaming head, Misty interjects, defending her man.

"Oh, this coming from you, Miss 'I'll babysit from downstairs while the baby is upstairs.' Real responsible, Jayd." What did this heffa just say to me? And how did she know about my sleepwalking incident when I left Rah's daughter, Rahima, upstairs late at night while I walked downstairs, unaware that I was dreaming at the time? If my mom's neighbor Shawntrese hadn't woken me up, I don't know what would have happened to Rahima or to me. Luckily, Rah doesn't know about that, and Shawntrese doesn't remember because with my mom's and Mama's help, I erased all of Misty's evildoings from when she and Esmeralda decided to hijack my dreams during the holidays. But I guess Misty still remembers every damn thing. We'll have to work on that before Misty does unnecessary damage with her loose lips and hips working overtime these days.

"Misty, you don't know what you're talking about." That's all I can say without further incriminating myself. Nellie and Mickey look from me to her, wondering what they missed.

"Okay, here's what we're going to do," Mr. A says, rising from his seat and standing at the whiteboard behind him. "We'll have an actual runoff for all the officers next month. That'll give everyone plenty of time to think carefully about who should be in which position. So let's shoot for at least two nominees for each office."

"That's a great idea, Mr. Adewale," Emilio says, the best teacher's pet ever. "We should also consider a logo for our club. I've taken the liberty of sketching down a few ideas." He stands up behind his desk next to the teacher's and passes the sketch pad to a visibly impressed Mr. A, who looks over the drawings carefully before commenting.

"Very talented, Emilio. And I like your initiative."

If I didn't know better, I'd say Emilio was gunning for president, when just a couple of weeks ago he was rooting for me to claim the throne. I guess he's not completely over the rejection I served him for kissing me without my permission. It's not my fault he came on too strong and self-righteous for me. And I see I was on point about his ego after all.

"Thank you, Mr. Adewale." Mr. A passes around the sketch pad of ideas about how we should represent ourselves. When the pictures finally make it to me, I look at them carefully, noticing that Emilio conveniently left out my deity, Oshune. From what I can see, most of the images are of the main orishas, with an outline of the African continent in the background, but the rest of the club members don't know, nor could they care less. To them, they're black superheroes, and, so far from their reactions, they like what they see.

"Ah, man, these are tight," KJ says, passing the pad around to the rest of his crew. "The black man and woman together—man, that's where it's at," he says, looking dead at me. If staying so-called "true to my race" means I have to date these idiots, I guess I am the sellout everyone's calling me. That's why Emilio left out Oshune—because he knows she's the only female orisha who knows no boundaries and is as powerful as any of the male orishas alone or all together.

"Okay, there's the bell for fifth period. We'll continue this discussion next week, and be ready with your nominations." Ready's right. I'll be damned if Emilio and KJ take over this club when it was my idea, sneaky bastards. I know Emilio's new to the game, but he's acting like an old player. We each gather our lunch trash and other belongings, ready to get the last two classes of the day over with.

"I like your drawings, Emilio. Have you been sketching the orisha very long?" I ask, easing into my threat. He needs to know I'm not afraid to go up against him or anyone else who tries to keep me from my spot. I didn't really want to be president, but now that it's officially up for grabs, I want it bad. Misty's conniving ass can wait until I get home. I'll give her a piece of my mind in private.

"As long as I can remember," he says, grabbing his backpack and sketch pad before leading the way out of the classroom. I have only four minutes and counting to make it down the hill to the drama room, so I'd better make this quick. We both wave good-bye to Mr. A, who is caught up in conversation with Misty about her tardiness. I'm glad someone else is tired of her trifling ways.

"I noticed you didn't include Oshune in the pictures. Any particular reason why, when you and I both know that without her there is no life at all?" Emilio stops in his tracks and looks down at me, thinking carefully before responding. I guess he's trying to find the right words because English isn't his first language.

"You know, Oshune is sweet, but she's also very promiscuous," Emilio says, the words rolling from his tongue like the gospel truth it isn't. "I think we should choose a more dignified female deity like Yemoja or Oya to honor, along with the male orishas, to balance it all out." He obviously didn't take enough time to choose his words, because he just ignited a fire in me I didn't know existed.

"What did you just say about my mama?" I don't care what Emilio's first language is—he knows those are fighting words. If it's one thing I can't stand, it's when someone talks about my mothers, both spiritual and physical.

"Jayd, I did not mean to offend you. I know how sensitive Oshune's daughters are, which is another reason I think we should choose someone else." Emilio's thick Spanish accent has completely lost its charm. I wish he would shut up, but he's on a roll this afternoon. "We are trying to set a certain standard with the African Student Union that I don't think you understand quite yet. We can discuss this more later," he says, leaving me shell-shocked as he walks toward his class. What kind of standard does he think we're trying to set, and why wouldn't I understand it, being that it was my idea in the first damn place? I'm so pissed that if I still had Maman's—my great-grandmother's—powers like I did when Reid came at me with his arrogant bull about the formation of the club a few weeks ago, Emilio would be squirming on the ground by now like the snake he is. Mama took my powers from me, saying that I wasn't ready to keep them, even though they were left behind from one of my dreams. But wait until I tell Mama about Misty's apparent memories of stealing my powers, coupled with Emilio's disrespect of our lineage. I know she's going to feel my fire and hopefully help me chill out before it gets out of control.

When I make it to the beauty shop after school, Mama and Netta are in their own world, which is the usual when it's just the two of them. Mama and Netta are like twins separated at birth; both are powerful women in their own right, but together they are unstoppable, and they know it. Mama and Netta stop their chatting to greet me and get right back to their exciting conversation about this past weekend's ceremony for Netta's son, Jeremiah. I can't help but be calm when I'm in their collective aura.

The homemade vanilla-and-almond-scented candles burning throughout the quaint yet open space soothe my frayed nerves and welcome me to the communion that is Netta's Never Nappy Beauty Shop. Emilio's pompous ass really works me up. I don't even remember what happened in my drama or my weight-lifting classes. All I could think about was my pounding headache from my dream last night, which was made even more apparent by the cold blow Emilio served up about our mother, Oshune, after the ASU meeting. I didn't even get to ask him if he's thinking about running for club president, and I hope the answer's no. That position is rightfully mine, and no matter what my haters may think of me, everyone knows I'm the best woman for the job, and I'm willing to fight for it if I have to.

"How's Jeremiah doing, Ms. Netta?" I ask while placing my work apron over my head, ready to get busy. Netta's the one in the client's chair for a change but is still in control of the conversation. She usually does her own hair like we all do, but today is a special treat for her. Mama's returning the weekly treat of having her hooked up by a talented stylist, like a real friend should—although I'm sure there's more to it than that. Usually, if Mama has to do Netta's hair, it's because of a spiritual cleansing needed for either Netta or herself.

"Girl, he's fine, except for the fact that he's always asking me for money, like I'm the Bank of Compton," Netta says, making Mama laugh more out of empathy than because it's funny. Mama has the same issue with her children. "That boy tens-and-twenties me to death. But, hopefully, now that he has Baba Shango in his corner, he will keep up with his own money and give me back some of mine, too."

"I know that's right," Mama says, taking the two hot curlers and single flatiron out of the miniature oven sitting at the station next to Netta's work space. It's rare for Mama to work with hair tools anymore, unless she's cleaning them. I need to take notes, but my memory will have to do the trick. "How was your day, baby?" Mama asks, redirecting the conversation my way, and I'm grateful. I need to get today out of my head—literally. The knot from my fantasy fall is still throbbing, reminding me of today's lingering drama.

"It was okay except that I had to defend Oshune against Emilio's simplification of her as solely a sex goddess," I say, collecting all the dirty towels near the sinks to wash. On Mama's Tuesdays—when she's the only client allowed in the shop—we're able to get the majority of our housekeeping chores done for the week, laundry included.

"Who is Emilio again?" Netta asks as Mama parts Netta's hair, ready to flatiron and curl it. Netta's got the thickest naturally auburn hair I've ever seen. She likes to keep it short, but it's still very full and looks gorgeous when it's loosely curled all over her head, like Mama's probably planning on doing now.

"Emilio is the new exchange student from Venezuela who's

also a child of Orunmilla, remember?" I say, reminding her of how that arrogant boy came into my life. I have enough problems without the added pleasure of dealing with a stranger's issues.

"Oh, the little boy who had a crush on you," Mama says, recalling our brief conversation about Emilio before I found out that he was a grandmama's boy. If his *abuelita* said the sky was orange, he'd never question it as the gospel truth.

"Well, doesn't he know that Orunmilla was one of Oshune's husbands? If she was good enough for his daddy, I know she's good enough for that little fool, talking bad about our mama like that," Netta says, moving her head to the right so Mama can get to the hair in the back of her head. "He should be ashamed of himself."

"Everyone always talks about Oshune being sexual and all that," Mama says, now guiding the flatiron expertly through Netta's short tresses. It looks so relaxing to sit in Mama's chair. The last time Mama did my hair, I couldn't even speak. "That's a watered-down version of our mother, to say the least. She is pure love and joy, all the good things in life. And that, my dear, is what it's all about."

"Not this madness that y'all young fools deal with these days," Netta says, supporting Mama like the true homegirl she is. I wish I had one tight friend like Mama does in Netta. Where are my homies, for real?

"I'm not part of that, 'y'all,' " I say, defending myself against the ignorance of some of the people in my generation. I call them fools, too, even if, technically, they are my peers.

"I know that, little Jayd," Netta says, waving her hand at my necessity to speak up. "It's your little friends I'm talking about, like Mickey and Nigel, not to mention Misty and that little pretty boy she's messing with." As a hairdresser, Netta knows about everyone's business even if most of it is second-hand information. Misty's mom's best friend still gets her hair done by Netta, although I've never run into her here, and I hope that never happens. "Boys don't know how to court girls, and girls don't know how to make boys work for it anymore. You better not turn into one of these fast-ass little girls who live with men before they get married, like—" Netta stops short of saying my mother, because she knows my mom could be listening, via my thoughts, and doesn't want to hurt her feelings, especially since she's turned her life around since she was my age.

"It doesn't always work out bad," I say, ready to defend my mom. She always seems to be the example of what not to do, but if you ask me, my mom's done pretty well for herself, considering she's a divorced, single mother living in the hood, and she should be applauded for that. "My mom and Karl practically live together, and they're engaged." Mama looks at me as if to say "please" but softens her stance about her eldest child's decisions in life and love, mostly because we all have a good feeling about Karl.

"There are exceptions to every story, but don't believe the hype, Jayd," Mama says, pointing the small curlers at me, directing me to gather the towels at her station to add to the already full load in the basket I'm carrying. "Don't get caught up in other people's versions of what love is or what's right or wrong in life. You have to figure out those things on your own."

"I know you're right," I say, finally letting Mama win because she always does. I take the laundry to the wash area and load the linens into the machine. Thank goodness Netta's husband is a contractor. Netta has made this shop her home away from home, with a small service porch off the wash area along with a bathroom and kitchenette, too. The back of the shop is where a private bathroom and the office/shrine room are located, which is where Mama spends most of her time while customers are here. Mama doesn't like to deal with gossiping clients, especially because a lot of the talk is about her. "That's why I'm not rushing into anything serious," I say as the memory of Jeremy and me making out comes to the front of my mind. I hope Mama didn't catch that one.

"Not yet. But when you meet the right one and it's the right time, mark my words, all bets will be off," Netta says, eyeing her hair in the mirror before Mama puts the final touches on her style. Netta looks good and refreshed. I take the bucket of clips out of one of the cabinets at Netta's station and begin collecting the silver clips to wash. There's always something to do around here. It's a wonder they didn't hire me to help sooner.

"I hear you, Ms. Netta." I haven't told either one of them that I'm dating Jeremy exclusively now, but I have a feeling Mama already knows, and I don't want to hear it. She's never been a fan of me dating Jeremy, for all the obvious reasons—because she has a soft spot for Rah.

"Careful with these boys, Jayd," Mama says. "We've already seen Rah's temper, and you know where Jeremy comes from with his racist daddy and all," she adds, reminding me that Jeremy and his brothers can date girls from different races, as long as they don't bring home any mixed babies, which is why Jeremy gave up knowing his own child by his ex-girlfriend Tania, who should be delivering their baby very soon. Unlike what Mama and Netta are saying, Tania's wealthy family made sure she was married off and living in New York. Mickey's shooting for a similar happy ending, no matter how delusional it may be. Hell would freeze over before Mrs. Esop would let that happen.

"Get to know their families better to get a more complete picture of the person you're befriending," Mama says. I don't know how fair it is to judge a dude by his family. I know she's not talking about Rah, because Mama knows his father's parents very well, and they outweigh his mom, who's a stripper, and his father, who's a good guy but got caught up and is now serving life in prison.

"I wonder what would be said about me if more people got to know my family?" I think aloud, seriously pondering that notion. With the rare occasion that Rah and Jeremy have come over, no one really chills at Mama's house. It's never been allowed with any of her children or with me and Jay. It's not really a spoken rule as much as it's just understood that we don't bring people home unless it's a special occasion. That fact alone says a lot about what others must think of the James household. That's why Rah and I have been friends for so long, even when he acts like a complete jackass. He understands how we roll around here and never judges me.

"Who cares what your little so-called friends think. With friends like yours, you don't need any enemies," Mama says, combing Netta's hair. I know Netta knows how blessed she is to have Mama in her head. Mama doesn't do anyone's hair anymore, not even mine, but Mama follows divinations to the letter, and if doing Netta's hair is what the orisha told her to do, it's as good as done.

"Too bad she's got those, too." Netta's got that right. And the fact that my friends and my enemies alike are working my nerves has got me all twisted up.

"Yeah, I do. And now they all seem to be ganging up on me for one thing or another. And my friends don't even remember my birthday or care about the sacrifices I've made for them." Mickey's really outdone herself this time.

"Girls can lust, too, Jayd. It's not just boys who want everything you're willing to give them. Lust takes and love gives. Haven't I told you that a million times?" I know Mama's right about that. Sometimes girls are worse than the boys. "And with these little frenemies you're running around with, like Misty and Mickey, it's a wonder you haven't been killed."

"Mama, it's not that serious," I say, running hot, soapy

water in one of the three washbowls to soak the hundreds of clips I've collected. With any luck I'll get off early tonight and get some studying done. Tomorrow is our first practice exam for the English AP in second period, and I want to do well.

"Oh, but it is, sweetie," Mama says as Netta takes the hot curlers out of the miniature oven and places them on the white towel to cool. She can't help doing her job, even when she's not technically the one working. "Emilio got close to you under the guise of friendship, and now he's turned on you, just like the other frenemies in your life."

"So how do I protect myself when anyone could be a potential enemy?" This is too much to deal with tonight. "Why can't a friend just be a friend?"

"Jayd, that's like asking why do people die. The world's a cold, harsh place at times, and that is why you need to always protect yourself in every way possible, even from the people who claim they love you." Mama's right on point with that one. I've been feeling down all day because two of my closest friends think I've betrayed them, when in actuality it's my trust that's been betrayed.

"You're right, and I'm going to change this madness sooner rather than later," I say, feeling more confident than I have all day. My headache has even lessened. Mama and Netta can make the most difficult problems seem so simple.

"If nothing else, I know you're a fighter for justice, and assassinating our mother's character is the same as attacking us personally. Don't let that little fool get away with that, especially if he's a true devotee like he claims to be. Emilio had better recognize he's fighting a losing battle talking bad about you and your lineage," Mama says, spraying Netta's finished do with hair sheen. Damn, Mama's got skills.

"That's right, little queen," Netta says, smacking on her Big Red gum louder than usual, she's so excited about her fresh hair. Mama gives Netta a look in the mirror, and she slows her roll a little bit. They smile at each other, both satisfied with the reflection in the large lighted mirror at the station.

"Your visions are here to help you, even if they do hurt sometimes," Mama says, alluding to my head injury and other battle wounds from past dreams. "You stand on the shoulders of all the women who came before you, and you have all your ancestors' and Orisha's love and support. Never doubt yourself or your power."

They're both right. There's no way Emilio can beat me in a presidential campaign for ASU or in a character debate about Oshune. Who the hell does he think he is telling me about myself? Like Oshune, I can be as giving to my friends as a lake full of fish is to a fisherman on a spring morning and as dangerous as that same lake on an ice-cold winter's night. Which side of my personality surfaces is contingent upon what's necessary, and, right now, self-preservation calls for a cool head. That starts with me doing my work—absolutely no distractions allowed.

~ 3 ~
All-Nighter

*"Gonna be a long night, it's gonna be all right/
On the night shift."*

—THE COMMODORES

"**K**eep staring into his eyes, that's it. Don't let anything distract you, not for a second," Mama whispers over my shoulder, watching my eyes as I stare into my father's sleepy browns. "Now think what you want him to think, say what you want him to say." I look into my father's eyes, now sharing his thoughts.

"It's cold in here, Mama," I say, but I don't sound like myself. I have my mother's voice, which can only mean that I'm dreaming as her again. Oh hell no, this isn't good. The last time I saw with my mom's powers, I went blind—yet another side effect from Misty's unfortunate claim over my dreams. That was a cold night, and I don't want to go back there again.

"Yes, the mind is naturally a cool place. It is the world around us that makes it hot." Mama touches my shoulders with both her hands and leans in closer, moving my body to align perfectly with my father's. He's across the small backyard, eating corn on the cob and talking with his friends. And from the feel of it, my mom likes what she sees, sort of how I feel when I see Jeremy walk, run, or do anything else. Oh, this is too weird.

"Okay, Mama, now what do I do?" Mama presses firmly

on my mother's shoulders and jumps into my mom's thoughts, now seeing as she sees. With both powers in my head, I can see everything my father's thinking, from how the food he's eating is too salty to how good my mom looks in her form-fitting, emerald sweater dress that sets off her eyes perfectly. "I'm glad I wore this," I say, smiling at my own taste. I see my mother hasn't changed one bit.

"Yes, chile, but you're missing the lesson as usual. Look and learn, Lynn Marie," Mama says, now speaking into my father's mind, all the while keeping his eyes locked on my mom's.

"Carter, you're going to ask me to the senior prom," Mama says, voicing what my mother has wanted for a while now, according to her eighteen-year-old memory. This must be right before my mom and dad were engaged and she abruptly moved out, leaving her powers behind because Esmeralda— our evil neighbor, Mama's nemesis, and Misty's spiritual godmother—stripped her of them out of jealousy. Esmeralda's an old-school hater of Mama's. They were best friends back in the days when they lived in New Orleans, but that all changed when they moved to Compton, and there's been a constant battle between them ever since. No wonder Mama's so happy to have Netta in her life. She knows the other side of friendship, and it's not a comfortable place.

"Carter, you are going to ask me to the senior prom," my mom repeats. I can feel my father's thoughts forming the same words, completely unaware that he's being mentally coerced into reaching a conclusion he was already thinking but not quite ready to act on. My mom basically made up his mind for him while my dad's thoughts are still cool— without the intrusion of other opinions from his friends or family. I'm sure my mom regrets that action now because he had a pregnant wife at home, and had she done her re-

*search through his family, she would have been forewarned.
But that's not the point of this lesson.*

*"And here he comes." Mama leads the way out of my fa-
ther's mind, unlocking her visual hold on him first, and
then my mother lets go, allowing my dad to follow through
with his action. It's nice to know my parents once liked
each other, before all the drama got in the way. As he makes
his way over to where we're standing by a tree near the barbecue grill, Esmeralda walks in through the gate. But when
she gets closer I see that it's actually Misty's spirit who has
entered my dream. Her cold blue eyes are glowing, and she
directs them straight toward my mother, knowing her icy
gaze has no effect on Mama.*

*"My head," my mom moans, the pounding in her head
mimicking the rush of cold blood surging through her veins.
My mom's head feels like a brain freeze times a million, and
Misty's loving every moment of it.*

*"Let go of my daughter, Esmeralda," Mama says, reclaim-
ing my mom's powers and marching right into Misty's head.
Mama quickly jumps into my father's head and sends him
to get something to drink from the cooler near the table he
was eating at. Mama's got the coldest powers I've encoun-
tered yet, able to borrow anyone's sight she needs at the
time. Now she fully focuses her attention on my mom, and
thank God, because my head can't take much more.*

*"Lynn Marie, she can't hurt you if you don't let her,"
Mama says, whispering into my ear, but I can barely hear
her because the noise in my head is so loud. "Remember
what you just felt in Carter's mind. That cool, calm feeling
is your power. Hold on to it, and Esmeralda's sight will
have no hold on you." So that's how Esmeralda got into my
mom's head when my mom left during a heated argument
with Mama. My mother was so pissed she literally couldn't*

see straight, and Esmeralda was there to seize the moment, breaking my mom down completely.

My mom thinks of the moment that just passed with my father and how easy it felt thinking his thoughts, redirecting that power to use on Esmeralda. Instead of attempting to close her eyes from Esmeralda's lethal stare, she returns the look like a mirror. My mom's eyes glaze over, no longer penetrable by Esmeralda's eyes via Misty, causing the cold blue stare to bounce back on its owner.

"That's it, Lynn Marie. You've got it. Don't be afraid of her," Mama says, letting go of my mother's shoulders and smiling at her progress. Misty's head is the one pounding now. Completely unaware of everything, my father drinks his water and decides to finish what he started a few moments ago.

"I love this," my mom says. Misty shivers at the boomerang effect of her cold blow. That's what happens when you throw energy out, whether good or bad—it's bound to come right back at you.

"Well, hello there, ladies," my dad says, unknowingly distracting my mom's attention and freeing her mental captive. Mama returns the greeting and chooses to leave my parents alone.

With Mama's telepathic departure from my mother's walk down memory lane, I sit up in my bed and turn off my alarm before it sounds. When it's this early, it's so quiet I can actually hear people on the next block performing their early morning tasks, and I can gather my thoughts. My mind is still cool from my mother's powers, and it's a good feeling. Too bad I can't stay this chill all day, but, hopefully, I can remember how good this place feels if Emilio, Misty, or anyone else gets on my nerves today. Mama says the most powerful thing a human being can possess is a calm, cool mind, and after the dream I just experienced, I feel her.

* * *

So far it's been an easy morning, as South Bay High goes. Mr. Adewale gave us a term-paper assignment in Spanish, due after spring break. I thought it was supposed to be a break, and the other twenty-five students in the class felt the same way. These teachers are serious about keeping their title of being a California Distinguished School. They crack the academic whip all the time, vacations be damned. And I'm so unprepared for our practice English AP exam during second period in a few minutes that if I could find some way out of it, I would. Unlike Jeremy and Mickey—the king and queen of ditching school—I have a mama who would kick my ass if I ever made a habit out of not only missing school but running away from a challenge.

My phone vibrates in my hand, and I flip it open. I don't wear a watch, so I use the pink cell as a clock between periods. I quickly read another text from Nellie that says she's going to meet me at Chance's house instead of riding there with me as we originally planned. I'm already regretting agreeing to go with her to Chance's house after school. Nellie sure does know how to get her way. Last night while I attempted to study after work, she texted me repeatedly until I agreed to be her personal cheerleader at the family dinner. If it weren't for Chance also requesting my presence, I probably wouldn't go. I had to give in if I wanted to get any studying done, which wasn't much by the time I got off the phone with her. I'll have to make up for my lack of proper studying tonight after dinner. I already requested this afternoon off from work and can't give up too much of my time for Nellie or anyone else.

Charlotte and her rich-bitch crew are already seated in the row of desks across from mine, ready for the exam. Even Alia looks content seated at the desk next to me. I take my seat and a deep breath, ready to deal with whatever comes of this test. I just want it to be over. The sooner Mrs. Malone gets in here, the better.

"Good morning, class," Mrs. Malone says, Mrs. Bennett walking in behind her. Doesn't she have her own class to teach? Every time I look up, the broad has got her hands up in someone else's mix. Then I see Jeremy walk in, and the rest of his class follows. I guess the Honors and Advanced Placement classes are joining forces today. Lucky me.

"Good morning, boys and girls," Mrs. Bennett says, sounding like she's hosting an episode of *Sesame Street* instead of an eleventh-grade English class. She's so fake a blind person could see straight through her.

"We're going to make space for Mrs. Bennett's class to take the exam with us. We will start in exactly one minute, so get comfy," Mrs. Malone says, directing the students to fill in the twenty or so empty seats in the room while Mrs. Bennett passes out the papers. The AP courses have about half the enrollment of other classes. Jeremy sits across the room, winking at me as he takes his seat. He opted out of the AP track last year, but it's not like he needs the extra stress. Jeremy's had straight As since elementary school and one of the highest grade point averages in the entire school. He can get into almost any college he wants to, as long as he does well on the SAT exams next year.

"And we'll stay through break to grade the exams," Mrs. Bennett says, being the bearer of bad news that she usually is. "Let's begin." Mrs. Bennett closes the door and looks at the clock. Like I said before, whatever the outcome, I just want it to be over.

Exactly fifty-five minutes from our start time, Mrs. Malone softly says, "Time," and we all put our pencils down. That was the most grueling exam I've ever experienced. Some of the words were completely foreign to me, and the concepts in the three short-essay questions were unfamiliar. I consider myself to be pretty intelligent when it comes to the English language, but this was definitely some strange shit.

"Please switch papers with the person to your right and pass your essay questions up to the front," Mrs. Malone says, turning on the projector near her desk, displaying the answers and grading scale to the multiple-choice questions. Mrs. Bennett collects the essays to start grading. After several minutes of quiet grading, we get to see our papers. I don't even want to know my grade.

"So, Miss Jackson, do you see why I didn't want you on the AP track?" Mrs. Bennett asks, returning my essay exam to me. "Quite honestly, I think it's very selfish of you to take another, more suitable student's place on the track, knowing all along you aren't worthy." Mrs. Bennett is smiling from ear to ear, which can only mean I didn't do too well on the practice exam—no surprise, but I really wanted to show her ass up.

"A two," I say, reading my grade aloud. I need at least a three to pass, and I'm sure I did better than this, but Scantrons don't lie, I guess. The grades for the essay questions are another thing altogether, and, knowing Mrs. Bennett, she didn't cut me any slack. Good thing she's not grading the real thing, or I'd really be screwed.

"Yes, a two. And to think, because of your financial dilemma, you don't even have to pay for the three exams you're scheduled to take, yet I'm sure you'll fail them all. What a pity," Mrs. Bennett says, walking out of the room as the final warning bell for third period rings, signaling the other students to leave as well. Talk about a hit and run. As I gather my backpack and purse to head to government class, I notice that everyone else seems real cool about their grades. Am I the only one who didn't get it?

"Don't worry, Jayd," Mrs. Malone says, propping herself up on the corner of my desk before I can make my escape. I feel so humiliated. The last thing I want is counseling from

the hippie teacher. "There are still several weeks left to prepare for the exams, and you're not far from passing at all.
You should also consider linking up with Alia and Charlotte
to attend as many study groups as you can between now and
then."

"Study groups?" I ask, rising from my seat. This is the first
I've heard of any study groups. They must have wanted them
to remain private, but if it'll help, I'll gladly crash that party.

"Yes, they meet at least once a week after school, off campus. And trust me, it helps. I have complete faith in your abilities no matter what, and believe in the No Child Left Behind
Act fully." I know she's trying to help, but her public-service
announcement isn't making me feel any better. But I will ask
Alia about her study crew during fifth period.

"Thanks, Mrs. Malone. I appreciate the information," I say,
meeting Jeremy by the door. He stuffed his exam into his
backpack without a second thought. Must be nice to be so
confident.

"Bye, kids," Mrs. Malone says to our backs as we walk out.
It's a good thing our government class is in the hall around
the corner. The warning bell for third period rang almost three
minutes ago, and Mrs. Peterson would take great pleasure in
marking us both late.

"So how did my girl do?" Jeremy asks, pulling me into his
embrace as we walk together. I put my arm around his waist
and allow myself to breathe in his soothing scent. Jeremy's
just what I need to make it through the long days up here.

"Not good at all. Mrs. Bennett's wicked ass made sure I
failed," I say, even though I know it's not all her fault. "I still
don't understand how you could like that bitch."

"She's not that bad," Jeremy says, looking down at me.
"She and my mom go way back. I guess I just see a different
side of her." Yeah, I guess he does.

"How far back do the Wicked Witch of the West and your mom go?" Mrs. Weiner also has it out for me, and I make sure I stay out of her way.

"Elementary school. They were in Louisiana together, and you already know South Bay is their alma mater, and that's where Chance's mom enters the picture." Witches traditionally travel in threes, but I've never met Chance's mom, so I don't want to jump to any conclusions. "I'm sorry, Jayd. I think I have something that'll make you feel better," Jeremy says, reaching into his right sweater pocket and pulling out a small pack of cinnamon doughnuts, my favorite. I have to be careful, now that we're back together. When Jeremy and I dated earlier this school year, I put on ten pounds just from our daily off-campus lunch ventures alone. I know he likes my thickness, but a sistah's got to stay healthy and fitting into her own jeans. With one homegirl pregnant and the other one almost down to a size two, I don't have the clothing options I used to via my friends' closets. Hell, I can't even wear Mickey's shoes anymore, her feet have stretched out so much. And Nellie's got thin model feet—the exact opposite of my short, fat *Flintstones* feet, as Rah would call them.

"Oh baby, you shouldn't have," I say, accepting the sweet treats. I open the plastic and stuff one bite-size circle into my mouth while entering the classroom. I'll try to sneak another in before Mrs. Peterson sees me. Jeremy kisses me on the nose before we take our seats. The bell rings loudly over our heads, and, finally, third period begins, and so does the rest of our day. I'm anxious to go to Chance's house this evening with Nellie for Chance's dad's birthday dinner; I also want to see what Chance's parents are like, especially because I already met them in my dream world on the day they adopted Chance—Christmas Day seventeen years ago. It's going to be a trip seeing them now.

* * *

As usual, there's a mad rush to get out of the gate in the parking lot after school. I should park in the lower parking lot by the drama room like Chance and Jeremy do most of the time, but I'll be damned if I have to hike up the hill leading from the theater area to my first-period class, which is near the main gate where I park. Chance already sent me a text saying he's waiting for us at his house already. I guess Nellie's rolling with Laura and the rest of the ASB crew since they have sixth period together and probably left early to go shopping or something. Chance rarely goes to his sixth-period art class, too. Am I the only one of my friends who believes in staying at school for the entire day?

Finally out of the lot and on my way to Chance's mini mansion in Palos Verdes, I catch traffic again and am forced to sit for a few moments while an accident clears on Pacific Coast Highway. My phone vibrates, and I see yet another text from Nellie. I'm giving this girl my phone bill next month because she is not in my network, and her neurosis is costing me a small fortune.

"I knew it," I say, voicing my frustration at the message and at the fact that I'm sitting still on this bright, sunny afternoon. Nellie's running late. I glance at the clock on the dashboard and pray that Nellie won't be too much later than I am. Alia gave me the information for the AP study group. They're meeting tonight at six to go over the exams and other information, and I don't want to be late. I already called Mama and asked her if I could stay out for the study session. She wasn't happy but agreed when I pointed out that I usually don't leave the shop until after nine, which is when I plan on driving home. Nellie owes me big-time for this one.

When I finally make it to PV, it's after four. I park in the U-shaped driveway and get out, making my way up the steep steps leading to the front door. Their Zen garden offers a stunning view and soothing sounds due to the large waterfall fixture to the right of the front door. These are the types of homes I see in magazines.

"Hey, Jayd. Thanks for coming," Chance says, letting me into his home before I can ring the doorbell. If I didn't know better, I'd say he was nervous. He gives me a hug and closes the front door before leading me inside. Last year Chance and I used to hang out here sometimes when his parents weren't home. I've missed this big-ass house. Jeremy lives around the corner, and so do a lot of the other PV kids. You know you've got hella bank when you can afford a crib around here.

"And you must be Jayd. I'm Mrs. Carmichael. It's nice to finally meet you. Have a seat," Chance's mother says, guiding me through the foyer while giving me a tight hug. Little does she know we've already met in my dream state and I know their family secret.

"My dad's running late at work, but he'll be here as soon as he can," Chance says.

Chance's mother walks ahead of us and into the formal dining room, heading straight for the chardonnay on the table. Chance and I sit down at the table on the same side, leaving an empty seat between us for Nellie. I see Mrs. Carmichael likes her liquor, just like Jeremy's mom. No wonder they're friends.

"Late for his own birthday dinner? I wonder who's keeping him this time," his mom says, pouring more wine. Before we can comment on the awkward moment, Chance's dad arrives. Now all we need is Nellie, and we can get this party started. I'm going to miss the actual meal, but I can lend my girl as much support as I can before I have to roll.

"Hey, babe, son, son's friend," Chance's father says, coming in from the kitchen and chewing on a roll. "Lindsey, what happened to the Benz this time? Do you know how much it costs to get a bumper fixed on an SL500?" He puts his brief-case on the dining room table, completely disregarding the careful placement of the napkins and china on the large marble table. This thing must weigh a ton, but I'm not a hater: the shit is flyy.

"It was a hit-and-run, David," Mrs. Carmichael says, now on her second glass. Where did the first one go that fast?

"Look here, I'll tell you what you're going to do," Mr. Carmichael says, sitting at one end of the table and chewing on his bread while talking at the same time. Talk about disgusting. "You kick in the door on the same side and call our insurance agency. Tell them to come tow it and give you an estimate. I'll bet they'll total it out and give you a check we can use as a down payment on another car."

Mrs. Carmichael looks like she wants to contest, but she doesn't. I can tell who's got the power in this house. Chance once told me his mother always wanted a large family but that his father allowed her to have only one child. Allowed. I wish Daddy would try to "allow" Mama to do something. The story would end completely opposite of Chance's family tale.

"But that's fraud, David, and, like the saying goes, we reap what we sow. Karma's real," Mrs. Carmichael says, looking sorry she ever told her husband about the fender bender. I agree with her. Playing with the universe is no joke. I wish Nellie would hurry and finish getting her hair done. This scene is making me uncomfortable, and she's the one supposed to be meeting the parents, not me.

"Karma is like voodoo," Chance's father explains, not knowing he's talking to a priestess. But I'll go ahead and let him continue. I want to see where he's going with this. "It can hurt you only if you believe in it. Look at George Bush. He's overseen the murder of tens of thousands of people, and he's playing golf on a ranch somewhere. Karma's one of those ideas hippies planted in the minds of weak people to make them think twice about doing the shit all the rich people are doing—i.e. us, babe." He takes a gulp of the red wine his wife just poured him, lets out a loud belch, and continues dictating. "Now go on and call the insurance agency. We'll get you a new Benz tomorrow, babe."

"Yes, dear," Chance's mom says, rising from the dinner table per her husband's command. She looks like a defeated puppy, retreating with her tail between her legs. What an ass her husband is.

"No sense in paying a deductible if we can total it out, right?" Mr. Carmichael looks at me for an ally. I guess he figures because I'm black I'll be down with the latest plot and scheme. Unlike him, I do believe in both voodoo and karma, and I'm not getting on the bad side of either one of them, for real.

"I'm going to call to check on Nellie. I don't know what's taking her so long," I say, avoiding his question. I rise from my seat and follow Mrs. Carmichael into the living room. I quickly send Nellie a text, telling her to hurry her ass up and get over here. Nobody gives a damn about her hair anyway. Mrs. Carmichael retrieves a bottle of wine from the minibar and refills her bottomless glass. After meeting her husband, I can see why she drinks. No response from Nellie. What the hell is taking her so long to get here? I'm ready to bounce, and if I leave now I can make it to the meeting on time.

"I don't always do what he says, you know," Mrs. Carmichael says, gazing out the picture window overlooking her plush green lawn. Their backyard is not as spacious as Jeremy's but is just as striking. I look around and realize she must be talking to me because we're the only two people present in the spacious room. Mrs. Carmichael turns around and looks at me, her eyes red from crying or too many sleepless nights, or maybe a combination of both.

"Sometimes I smoke outside when he's asleep," she says,

returning her gaze outside. "He told me to stop smoking cig-
arettes years ago, but I still sneak one in every now and then
just to spite him." Damn, that's deep. Killing herself to piss
off her man. No one said love was logical.

I don't know what to say to her. I feel like I should say I'm
sorry or something equivalent, but I'm equally convinced she
really doesn't want a conversation. She just wants someone
to listen.

"You're one of them, aren't you, Jayd?" Mrs. Carmichael
asks, still focusing on the rose garden in our view. There are
so many types of flowers out there she could be a florist. Her
home is so peaceful except for the man she married living inside it. Her question throws me a little, but I know what she's
referring to.

"One of what?" I ask, trying to throw off her scent, but she's
on it like a bloodhound. These Southern folks can spot a conjure woman from a mile away.

"It depends on who you ask. Rainelle Burton calls your
kind root workers; Jewell Parker Rhodes, voodoo priestesses.
Tina McElroy Ansa would call you a caul child, and I, I call
you a seer." Mrs. Carmichael looks at me and smiles, waiting
for my reply, but I don't have one. Ms. Toni would be impressed by her apparent knowledge of voodoo literature. It
just freaks me out even more to know she's read about
women like me and is already hip to the game. She probably
thinks I can read her mind or some shit like that. Little does
she know that's my mom's gift of sight, not mine.

"Where'd you get that idea?" I ask, taken completely off
guard by her question. I feel like I've just been outed, and by
a white woman, no less. See what happens when I do favors
for my friends? I end up getting scolded, and this is the last
thing I need right now.

"Don't be so coy, Jayd. Chance told me all about your little
witch-hunt episode at school a while back. He also said you

admitted to being a priestess." Mrs. Carmichael looks into my eyes, studying my facial expressions. For a moment, I think I can hear what she's not saying, like in my dream last night where I was my mother before she lost her powers.

"He did?" I ask, surprised Chance would say anything about me to his mom, especially about Misty calling me out a few months ago, which was the first time I decided to stand up for my lineage at school. It's been more tense around campus than usual for me ever since. "What else did he tell you?"

"Well, he told me about you the first day of school last year. He was very impressed by your acting capabilities. He thought he met his leading lady in you," she says, sipping her wine carefully so as not to spill any on her white carpet and gesturing for me to sit in one of the two oversize cream-colored chairs across from the matching couch. Damn, I thought I was almost out of here. I can hear Chance's father in the dining room still discussing with his son what he thinks his wife should do about her fender bender. I guess talking to me is better than going back in there, and I don't blame her. If Nellie doesn't arrive soon, I'm going to head out, dinner or not. I can't take too much more of Mr. Carmichael's ego; there's not enough room in this house for it and me.

"He's not the only one impressed. I've never met anyone better at improvisation," I say, looking down at my phone and praying that it vibrates soon.

"Yes, my son is quite the spontaneous one," she says, catching a memory as it comes. Did I just see that memory, too? I think a little bit of my dream stayed with me from last night. Mama already stripped me of using my ancestor's power once—now she'll surely want to take my mom's away from me as well. But maybe it'll go away by itself, like a residual effect more than a new development in my gift of sight. "He's been like that all his life." The sadness in Mrs. Carmichael's eyes is evident by the softness in her look. Her tone lowers as she recalls Chance's childhood, and I share her silent memories.

"I can only imagine Chance as a child," I say, lying aloud. I can pretty much see the picture of her son's first step forming in her head, and I also remember him as a newborn from my own visions.

"Can you? I think you can actually see him as a child," Mrs. Carmichael says, staring hard at me, which is making me uncomfortable. "My mind feels very cool all of a sudden. I remember this feeling from the seers back home." Having a cool head is one of the side effects of my mom's talent when she's in other people's minds. What does Mrs. Carmichael really know?

"Mrs. Carmichael, I don't know what you've heard, but it's not like that." I look over my shoulder toward the dining room, praying Chance will rescue me soon. I don't want to be rude, and I understand his mom needs a distraction, but I don't feel like being the court jester tonight.

"Oh no? Then what is it like? Because I have a feeling you know more than you're saying." Mrs. Carmichael takes a seat on the couch directly in front of me and continues. "Chance also told me what you said to him about having black blood."

"Does he tell you everything?" Damn, Chance is more talkative than I gave him credit for.

"Not everything. For example, he never told me he had a new girlfriend. And when he finally did tell me she wasn't you, I was quite surprised and disappointed." Mrs. Carmichael takes a large gulp of her white wine, now noticeably tipsy.

"Nellie is one of my best friends. You'll love her," I say, speaking up for my girl even though it's clear Mrs. Carmichael favors me as her son's choice. The last thing I need is for another homegirl to accuse me of trying to get in good with her boyfriend's mother. Mickey's already gone off enough about that. The truth is, I'm usually the one mothers hate; Carla and Mrs. Weiner—Rah and Jeremy's mothers—are prime examples of that fact. KJ's mom liked me, but KJ was an ass, so I'm not counting that lapse in judgment.

"I don't know about that," she says, glancing at her Rolex, which matches Chance's Christmas gift from last year. These two really are close. "Punctuality is a characteristic I hold in high esteem." The doorbell rings, saving me from this conversation, and just in time, too. I was looking for an escape route. Finally, Nellie's here, and she can take the night shift because I'm out. Chance races to the front door from the dining room and opens the door for our girl, but it's not exactly the girl we were expecting.

"I'm so sorry I'm late, baby," Nellie says, walking in and shocking everyone by more than her tardiness. No, this trick didn't go dye her hair blond. Mrs. Carmichael and I walk into the foyer to greet the guest we've all been waiting for.

"Oh my," Chance's mother says upon seeing Nellie's new do. Oh my? Is she serious? What I know she really meant to say is the same thing that's going through my head.

"What the hell did you do to your hair?" I ask my girl. Has she completely lost her mind? Nellie's bright smile folds into a scowl. She looks like she's going to cry, and I immediately feel bad for my outburst. I didn't mean to embarrass her, but she should've given me a little warning, for real. I just saw her at school a couple hours ago and wasn't expecting this to walk through the door. Chance kisses Nellie on the cheek and closes the door behind her.

"This is for your husband," Nellie says, stepping inside the dining room and allowing us all to get a better look at her. I can see it's mostly a weave because I know what to look for, but she also dyed her real hair blond, too. What was she thinking?

"So you heard about my husband's love for cognac. Nice

gift," Mrs. Carmichael says, eyeing the bottle of brown liquor like it's a dirty pair of panties Nellie just threw in her husband's face, who's enjoying the show. Chance's parents are faded and the jealousy is really starting to show from Mrs. Carmichael. Unfortunately, I can hear every word she's not saying about Nellie, and it ain't pretty. Damn, that's some serious hating, and on Mr. Carmichael's birthday, too. "I'm very interested to know how a sixteen-year-old was able to purchase such an elite bottle of liquor."

"My dad likes cognac, too," Nellie says, taking a seat next to Chance, but I remain standing so I can make it out the door that much faster once I say my good-byes. "He gave it to me to give to you, Mr. Carmichael. Happy birthday." Chance's father smiles at Nellie, taking a large cigar out of the gold box on the dining table and lighting it.

"Well, it's nice to meet you, girl, and thank you for the drink. It'll go to good use," he says, laughing at his wife's obvious disdain for Nellie. "Let's eat."

"I hate to leave before the actual dinner, but I've got a study group to attend," I say, waving. "It was a pleasure, and thank you for having me."

"No, the pleasure was all ours, dear," Mrs. Carmichael says, walking from the minibar next to the entryway and giving me a hug and kiss on the cheek. Nellie's anything but happy to see her boyfriend's mother's affection for me. Here we go again.

"Yeah, Jayd, thanks for coming," Chance says, rising from the table to walk me out, but Nellie snatches his shirt, forcing him back down. So much for me being helpful to my friend.

"You come back and visit us soon, Jayd. I mean that." Mrs. Carmichael looks sad as she closes the door behind me. I can hear her regret at my departure loud and clear in my mind. My mother's gift of sight allowed her to do more than just see in people's heads—she can also cool their thoughts and provide them comfort. What a beautiful gift to have. I see now why Mama was so distraught her daughter lost it: we're all healers in some way, and by giving up on her path, my mom also gave up a piece of our collective lineage. Maybe there's a way we can salvage my mom's sight through my own visions, but that'll have to wait for another day. Right now it's all about saving my own ass, and passing the AP exams is top on my list.

After not having dinner last night, I met up with the study group, but it was almost over by the time I arrived. I guess even with the APs around in six weeks, the South Bay High crew still doesn't miss an episode of *Beverly Hills, 90210*. My mom says it was the same way when the show was on back in her high school days. And for these rich folks up here, it must be like looking in the mirror. Alia even said the original show was filmed at another high school in the South Bay area. It must be nice to live the life so many envy. The group is meeting again after school, and I'm glad for it, even if I'm not pleased with the location.

Charlotte, who undoubtedly volunteered her house so she can show off her daddy's fortune, is hosting tonight's study session. I can't stand her ass, but if I'm going to pass these tests with flying colors, I've got to suck it up and deal.

"Shit," I say, looking down as my travel speakers for my iPod fall between the car seats. The next time I have some extra cash, I'm buying a radio for this ride. I've gotten pretty good at mastering my mom's stick shift, but these steep hills in Redondo Beach are a killer. I make my way up the winding road and look at the addresses for Charlotte's house. All the lawns are perfectly manicured, with various alarm signs posted near the picturesque flower beds present in each one.

When I arrive at the correct residence, I find a spot that's almost level, so I don't have too much trouble parallel park-

ing, even though it's several houses away from my destination. I'm not ashamed of my mom's car, but parking it in the
same driveway as the BMWs, Mercedes, and Audis the other
students on my AP track drive doesn't make me feel my best.

I finally reach Charlotte's house and ring the doorbell.
Her next-door neighbors eye me carefully before they step
out of their black Range Rover, probably wondering what I'm
doing here, which is none of their damn business. I ring the
bell again, and this time a woman in a black-and-white maid's
uniform answers the door. I didn't know people actually wore
the blouse-and-skirt combination with the headgear and
apron to match, aside from on Halloween.

"May I help you?" the Latina sister asks, also surprised by
my presence.

"I'm here for the study group," I say. She looks me up and
down, sizing up my Old Navy jeans and Baby Phat long-sleeved
shirt, focusing on the large gold bamboo hoops hanging from
my ears. When she sees my Lucky bag, her stern face softens
a bit, now satisfied that I'm not an imposter, I suppose.

"They're in the great room," she says, gesturing straight
ahead of us to what looks like a living room. Great or not,
I'm sure it's the same thing.

"Did anyone bring any coffee? Our maid forgot to drop by
Starbucks this morning, and my daddy's gourmet brand is
off-limits. Good help is so hard to find these days," Charlotte
says, loud enough for their employee to hear, who is still behind me, making sure I don't swipe any of the expensive dec-
orative art on the round table in the foyer. I step down a
single step into the most spacious room I've ever seen in person. Now I see why they call it great. Her living room sits off
a cliff overlooking the ocean. The glass doors and windows
lining the wall allow me to fully absorb the breathtaking
view. I don't even want to know what the rest of the house
looks like, for fear I might secretly become a hater.

"I'll go and pick it up now, Miss Charlotte," the house-keeper says, closing the door. Charlotte looks at me and smiles, satisfied that the fact that I've shown up to her multi-million-dollar home is a symbol of my acceptance of her superiority. Whatever. Let's just get on with it already. The sun is already setting, and we have work to make up from last night and new territory to cover before it's all said and done. Mama's less than happy that I'm missing work again for a study session, but what can I say? I need the help, and if this is how I can get it, so be it. I also didn't have a chance to tell Mama that I've retained some of my mom's powers, although they seem to come and go when they please. I tried using them today when Nellie started hating on me about reacting to her hair last night, but I couldn't shut her up with my thoughts, so I had to use my mouth instead.

"Come on in, Jayd. We're just about to get started," Charlotte says. I wave to the other fifteen or so students in the room and claim a space on the comfy couch, placing my backpack and purse next to me. Ella, Seth, and Matt are in attendance, and I'm shocked. With the auditions for the spring musical coming up in May, I'm surprised they let themselves leave the theater for a night. But I guess everyone needs to pass these exams. Charlotte's girls Laura and Cameron are also present, solidifying the bitch crew's presence in the room. "Oh, Consuela, could you be a dear and pick us up some snacks, sparkling water, and more pens? It looks like we might be here all night, and we should be prepared," Charlotte calls after an already frantic Consuela, who looks like she's trying to get away as fast as she can.

"Yes, Miss Charlotte," Consuela says, grabbing her coat from the hall closet before opening the front door. What a job it must be working for mini bitch and her family.

"Hey, Consuela, how's it going?" Jeremy asks, surprising Consuela and me both. What's he doing here? His AP days are a thing of the past. The homework apparently interfered with Jeremy's surfing schedule, though, being the golden child he is, he still gets all the love from the AP teachers, even if he is not on the Advanced Placement track.

"Oh, just fine, Mr. Jeremy. It's nice to see you again." Jeremy holds out one arm of her jacket so she can slip her arm through and complete her escape, shutting the antique wooden door behind her.

"What's up, people?" Jeremy asks, entering the great room and tossing a pound of French roast coffee Charlotte's way; she clumsily allows it to fall to the ground.

"Jeremy!" Charlotte shouts, picking up the bag and inspecting it for damage. "You're lucky it didn't bust. Otherwise, Consuela would have a very hard time getting grounds out of my daddy's prized Persian rug."

Jeremy shakes his head at her vanity and spots me sitting all alone on the love seat across the huge room. "Fancy meeting you here, Lady J," he says, walking over to me as I move my things down to the floor so he can sit.

Now I'm looking forward to this session more than ever. "Funny. I was just thinking the same thing," I say. Jeremy makes himself comfy next to me and kisses me in front of my classmates, causing Charlotte to become unnecessarily agitated.

"Excuse me, Jeremy," Charlotte says, placing the bag down on the long glass table she and several other students are seated at, including her girls—like they're Supreme Court judges. "But you're not on our track this year, or has your pot-induced coma finally taken over your memory?" Ooooh, it sounds like there's some historical drama between these two. I'll have to get the lowdown later.

"Don't get all bent out of shape, Charlotte. I've decided to take the APs this year after all."

"But you haven't been in the classes all year. How's that

even possible?" Candace, another misplaced AP student from our speech class, asks. I'm with her—how is it possible?

"Taking the courses isn't mandatory for test participation, counselor. Besides, Mrs. Bennett and my mom ganged up on me after the practice exam Tuesday, so here I am," Jeremy says, turning his baseball cap backward, ready to study. As intelligent as he is, he'll probably get a five on any exam he chooses to take. It must be nice to be a genius without too much effort. Unlike him and the rest of the students on my track, I haven't been prepping for standardized tests all my life.

"Whatever. Let's get started, please," Charlotte says, sitting down at the head of the table and announcing our schedule for the evening. I love that they're serious about their time. My friends could learn a thing or two from this uptight crew. "All in favor of starting with economics, moving on to history, and then finishing with English, please raise your hand." Everyone's in agreement, and we all retrieve the proper study materials.

"So, just like that, you're taking the Advanced Placement exams?" I whisper to Jeremy, who's opening a fresh spiral notebook for his notes. He pulls a mechanical pencil from behind his ear, ready to work.

"Just like that," he says, smiling his bright whites at me and winking. "I didn't object too much, because I knew my girlfriend would be at the study sessions, and because she's always working, I thought it might be a good way for us to spend some quality time together." Jeremy zips up his backpack and kisses me on the cheek.

"I hope she knows how lucky she is," I say, leaning over and returning the quick peck before we get too far off into microeconomics, which everyone present specializes in. If nothing else, we all have a love of our money in common.

"I think she's getting the idea," Jeremy says, kissing me

again but this time on the lips. Jeremy hasn't mentioned his "I love you" slip from last weekend, but I want him to know I feel the same way. When I'm ready, I'll say it back to him, but now is not the time or place.

"Okay," Cameron says, equally annoyed as her homegirl. "That's enough, you two. Time is money." She's got that right, and time is also my ass if I get home too late, so we'd better begin. Mama's already pissed that I've cut back my weekday hours at Netta's so I can participate in this study group, especially after I begged them to let me work there. If I keep it up, Mama's going to get fed up, and that won't be a good thing for me at all. I don't want to hear her mouth any more than the earful I'm getting for not being there. But tonight I'm burning the midnight oil if need be, repercussions be damned. I just hope Mama understands.

~ 4 ~
Verbal Diarrhea

*"I may stay away for a night or two /
But all form of respect unto you is still due."*

—GREGORY ISAACS

By the time I make it back to Compton, it's well after ten. I know it's past my curfew, but I really enjoyed the healthy arguing and intellectual stimulation this evening. During class is one thing, where the teacher's in control of who gets to showcase his or her brilliance or lack thereof. But in a club our peers are the ultimate judges. It was like being surrounded by a bunch of young professors, each with his or her own theory about everything, and for the first time I was officially included in that group. By the time I left, to the rest of the students it was still too early to throw in the towel, but to my grandmother, anything after nine for me is ass-kicking time.

I park my mom's car across the street and choose to lock the door from the inside rather than arm the alarm like I usually do, just in case Mama's already sleeping. I'd rather risk someone breaking into the ride than Mama hearing me come in late, if I can avoid it. When I talked to her earlier she sounded tired. Hopefully, she gave in to her exhaustion, and I can get inside without any complications.

"Have you completely lost your mind, girl?" Mama says as soon as I open the back door, scaring me like the ancestors used to do when I was a child. Even for ghosts, they weren't as sneaky as Mama. I should've known she'd be up waiting

for me. How do I tell her I lost complete track of time studying and that turning off my phone was mandatory?

"You can't tell me shit, Jayd, because I know you know
better than that," she says, snatching the thought right out of
my mind. At least other teenagers get a minute to make up a
reasonable lie before getting caught. No such luck in this
house. "You're getting to be too much like your mother for
me."

"Mama, it's not what you think," I say, stepping fully into
the kitchen and shutting the door behind me. Lexi—Mama's
German shepherd gatekeeper—follows me inside to witness
the tongue thrashing she knows is coming. She may be the
canine, but I'm the one in the doghouse right about now.
Daddy and Jay are probably already in bed watching television before nodding off, and Bryan's at his night gig where
he hosts a cable radio show. My other uncles are who knows
where, and I'm glad for it. It's always embarrassing when one
of the men witnesses Mama cussing me out.

Before I can continue with my defense, Mama cuts me off.
I can feel the heat in her head rise, and because she's so hot,
Mama can't feel my mother's powers overcome my own, al-
lowing me into Mama's head.

"Jayd, you've got to get back on point." Mama's weary
green eyes are bright red with anger. I look past her rage and
into her mind's eye, hearing the concern in its voice for my
safety and spiritual well-being. She's worried I'm turning out
to be just like my mother—staying out late, running with a
group of friends she doesn't know, and getting too close to
my boyfriend. At the rate her blood is pumping, Mama needs
to calm down. All these emotions aren't good for her health.
I attempt to communicate calming thoughts to her, but her
mind is resistant to my persuasion. Mama's still too pissed to
hear me inside; my young talents can't manipulate her mind.

"We have a lot of work to do, and I don't have time for

your teenage foolishness, you hear me?" I nod my head in submission, and Mama rises from the kitchen table and goes into the room we share. I feel bad for making Mama worry, but I think her unease is more out of control than of real concern for my safety. I hope she didn't catch that one. Thank God Mama's spiritual wi-fi isn't as on point as it normally is, or I'd probably get slapped for that last thought.

I walk into the room and see Mama stripping my bed down to the mattress. Without another word, she walks past me and into the living room, throwing my covers and sheets onto the couch. I look at her with tears in my eyes and know better than to contest. Her head is completely cool now, and her mind made up. This isn't the first time Mama's put me on the couch, and I'm sure it won't be the last. Luckily, I'm used to sleeping on my mom's couch during the weekend, but I will miss my twin-size bed tonight. I'm not looking forward to the feel of the plastic-covered couch sticking to my arms. Every time I try to readjust my covers around my body on that damn thing, they slide all over the place, leaving me out in the cold. But what can I do? Mama can be as cold as ice when she wants to be, and this is obviously one of those times. It's after eleven, and I need my sleep. I'll worry about getting back in Mama's "top faves" tomorrow.

"There she goes again. Mmm-mmm-mmm. What a waste of talent," one of the church ladies says as I walk down the aisle. With my speech in hand, I'm ready to give the sermon. But instead of walking toward the pulpit, I'm moving away from it toward the door. I look around on my way out and see Mama and my mom crying under black veils as if they're at a funeral, which is the only reason I can imagine they would be in church. Who died, and why am I here?

"You know, they say she was a good girl until that boy came into her life, and then it was all over."

"Just like her mama before her and her great-grandmother with that white lover on the side. Those Williams women are always going after the wrong men," another woman chimes in. "At least her grandmother had the good sense to marry a pastor—too bad for him."

"Too bad for little Miss Know-it-All," one of the gossipers hisses. "But that's what you get when you think you're grown at an early age. You catch an early death." I stop in the aisle and look at the two women still running their mouths, completely ignoring my existence. I backtrack to where my mom and Mama are seated, begging for some attention from them, but nothing. What the hell is going on here?

"Jayd, it's time," a voice from outside the church says to me, but I'm not ready to go—not until they acknowledge I'm here. It can't be my funeral, because I'm up and walking, or am I? Ignoring the voice's plea, I run back to the pulpit and look inside the open casket. I have never understood funerals like these where you can see the body all made up, and this corpse is especially disturbing—it's me with a smile plastered on my face. I try to scream, but I can't. Tears stream down my face as I reach inside the casket, touching my cold, lifeless hand. A tear drops from my chin to my corpse's cheek, causing her eyes to open. While they stare back at me, I notice they are no longer brown but green like all the other women in my lineage before me. What the hell?

"Jayd, it's time to get up," my uncle Bryan says, snapping me out of my dream. "And hurry up because I need you to drop me off at the bus station on your way to school. I'll be outside when you're ready." Damn, will he ever get his van fixed? And when did I become his personal taxi? I've got to put an end to his ride-mooching soon.

"I'm up," I say, placing my right foot on the carpet first and then the other, pushing the covers completely off me, allowing the morning air do its job waking me. Summer's less than three months away, and as far as I'm concerned, it can't come soon enough.

After a few moments of settling into this reality—post my disturbing fantasy world—I quietly make my way to Mama's bedroom and open the door. I still can't believe Mama made me sleep on the couch for coming home late from a study session. I seize today's wardrobe from the hangers on the back of the door and gently step back into the hallway, closing Mama's door behind me. Someone's already in the bathroom ahead of me this morning, which means it's not going to be a good day. I can handle Bryan and Jay going in before me because they clean up after themselves, but the rest of the fools in this house are worse than pigs in a sty.

I open the door to Daddy's room, trying not to disturb his and Jay's sleep while I retrieve my toiletries and other necessities out of the Hefty bags that double as my dresser drawers in their smallest closet. It must be nice to sleep until twenty minutes before the school bell rings. I honestly don't know what time Daddy wakes up, but it's not before me. Bryan and I are the early risers in this house.

Whoever's in the bathroom now has a hangover, just got home, or some of both. I'm so sick of my trifling-ass uncles, I don't know what to do.

The bathroom door opens as I exit Daddy's room, revealing the early-morning culprit. Everyone knows I get first dibs on the bathroom in the morning because I have to be at school—not that my uncles respect me much, but Mama laid down that law years ago, and it's been solid ever since.

My uncle Kurtis—the nastiest one of them all and also the biggest jerk—walks out of the steamy mess he left behind, smiling down sinisterly at me. I pass him by in the cramped hallway and brace myself for the work to be done. Cleaning up after a grown man is not the makings of a good morning.

"Damn, Kurtis. Will you ever learn how to put the shower curtain inside the tub while the water's running? It's common sense." I grab one of the funky towels in the overstuffed laundry basket and wipe the pool of water off the bathroom floor. This is why I make it a point to get in the bathroom before any of these fools—especially my Uncle Kurtis. Jayd Jackson is nobody's maid.

"Shut up and stop talking to me like you want to get socked in the mouth." I look at this big grown-ass fool and shake my head. I know better than to keep talking, but some days it's just too much for a sister to bear, living with all these men. If I learned how to clean from Mama, he should know better, too.

"Don't think I'm scared of you, punk, because I'm not," I say, attempting to close the bathroom door, but his big foot blocks my escape from the unexpected morning brawl.

"Go to hell, Jayd," my uncle says, attempting to get back inside, but I'm not budging. "You think you're better than a regular nigga, but you ain't no better than nobody."

"You go to hell!" I say, smashing Kurtis's foot in the door, but it's no use. His six-foot-five frame towers over my five-foot self any day. Finally forcing his way inside, Kurtis pushes me hard, and I push him right back, ready to throw down with him if need be. I haven't had to fight one of my uncles in years, but I haven't forgotten how.

"What the hell is going on out here?" Mama asks, coming out of her room and scaring us both. I should've been in and out of the shower by now. This bull has got to change, and now. Fighting with my uncle is not only a waste of my time but of my energy, too. I'm already tired from sleeping on the couch, and that, coupled with my regular Friday quizzes and other work, makes me even more irritated with my faulty start this morning.

"I can't do this anymore!" I yell at no one in particular.

"I'm tired of fighting with these grown-ass fools." I look directly at Kurtis, who looks like he wants to pounce on me. I wish he would. I'm so mad I'd bite the shit out of him in a minute.

"Little girl, you had better watch your tone and your language in my house," Mama says, her green eyes glowing with rage.

"Mama, how come you let Kurtis get away with being rude in your house, and I can't even study without getting reprimanded? It's not fair," I say, but I can tell by the hard look in Mama's eyes that she couldn't care less about my version of fair.

"I'm going to say this only one time, Jayd," Mama says in a low voice that gives me goose bumps. "As long as you live in this house, don't you ever curse at your elders—period."

"He's not my elder," I say, pointing at my stupid uncle, who's standing there with a smug look on his face. Mama always lets the boys get away with shit.

"In this house, Kurtis is still your uncle, and that means something, Jayd, no matter how foolish he may act."

Kurtis looks at Mama and laughs. Why do I even bother? They'll never get it, and I'm tired of trying to explain myself to them. For the first time this morning, my thoughts are calm, and I know just what to do to keep myself sane.

"I'm going to live with my mom." Did I just say that out loud? Apparently so, because Mama's eyes are redder than ever, but there's no taking the words back.

"You're not two, Jayd. Your little temper tantrum will get you nowhere you want to be, girl. Especially not with me." Mama shifts her weight from her right foot to her left and places her hands firmly on her full hips. Even in her cotton robe I can see how shapely she is. Mama's only a few inches taller than me, but that's all she needs to make me feel tiny in her presence.

"Jayd's become an ornery little wench, hasn't she, Lynn Mae? I guess because she's turning seventeen next week, she thinks she's grown now," Daddy says from his room. If I weren't so hurt by his bold words, I'd be shocked by his addition to the early-morning argument. At least he'll probably withdraw his invitation for me to speak at his church. I'm sure wenches don't give Easter Sunday sermons.

"I have to get to school before I'm late," I say, hoping she'll finally let me go. I can't take any more of their badgering. Mama looks into my eyes as hers take on an emerald glow of their own. Holding on to the visual lock, I remember my mom's dramatic departure from Mama's house as a teenager and her subsequent loss of powers—I learned this through Mama's vision. The last time I relived this moment, I lost my sight just like my mom. But it's different with me. I'm not leaving Mama because I don't love my skills; I need to leave to save myself, and that's a chance I'm willing to take, if my mom's on board with it.

"I already told you to watch your tone, girl," Mama says, visibly shaken by this ugly incident. How did this happen?

"Yeah, Jayd, watch your tone." Kurtis moves out of my way. I prepare to finally shut the door, ready to take a quick shower and bolt out the door, but Mama looks like she has something else to say, and I know better than to close the door on her.

"This isn't over, Jayd." Mama turns around and goes back in her room, closing the door behind her. I wish I could follow her and apologize, but I don't have time for that, and besides, none of this is my fault. At this rate I'll barely make it on time, and the last thing I want is to be late for my first class with Mr. Adewale.

After I shower and dress, I replace my belongings in Daddy's closet, noticing he's not in his bed. I guess after all the excitement he couldn't go back to sleep. There's no time for cereal, so a banana from the fruit bowl will have to do.

"Girl, what's gotten into you this morning?" Daddy asks as I try to make my way out the kitchen door; he walks in from outside with a Bible in his hands.

"I don't know, Daddy. I'm just frustrated and tired, I guess," I say, leaning against the open door. I feel more tired than when I woke up this morning.

"I hope you think carefully about the type of young woman you want to become. It starts now, and so far, so good until this morning," Daddy says, lifting my chin with his free hand and kissing me softly on the forehead. "Think carefully about what you want to say in front of the church on Easter Sunday."

"You still want me to speak?" I ask, surprised he's not rebuking me for mouthing off this morning.

"Of course I do, Tweet—now more than ever," Daddy says, pulling a ten-dollar bill out of the leather-bound book and handing it to me. "Gas." I love my granddaddy, and he's a sweet man. I know he and Mama have their fair share of problems, but his being a good provider isn't one of them.

"Thank you, Daddy. I'll talk to you later," I say, walking out the door and closing it behind me.

"I look forward to it. Be careful," Daddy says through the closed door. I'm glad he's not holding my words against me. That's one good thing about family: You can show your ass, and they'll still love you. Lexi, Mama's loyal pet, is asleep in her usual spot at the bottom of the steps. What a life this dog has.

When I get to the car, I see Bryan's not there yet. He's got the two minutes it takes for my mom's Mazda to warm up before I leave him wherever the hell he is. I walk across the street and open my ride, ready to roll. But before I can get in the car, I see Misty leaving Esmeralda's house. I still can't get over the fact that she and her mom stay with their evil godmother from time to time. Since Misty's grandmother died, she and her mom have had a pretty rough time, and as high as the cost of living is in Los Angeles, I'm sure they'll be struggling for a while. I kind of feel sorry for her, but having too much sympathy for Misty is dangerous for me.

"Good morning, Jayd," Misty says, switching her wide hips down the porch steps and closing the wrought-iron gate behind her. We wouldn't want the cats, birds, hamsters, chickens, and various other animals that call that condemned porch of Esmeralda's home to escape.

"Misty," I reply. It's hard to be polite to someone who tried to steal my dreams from me, which reminds me I need to grill her real quick about what she remembers from that unspeakable experience. "You'd think after you got your ass spiritually kicked, you'd be a little nicer to me, but I guess not, huh?" I ask, now that she's only a few feet away from me across the street. Misty better be careful on her way to school because in that outfit she could be mistaken for a hooker.

"Whatever, Jayd. That was one battle, but the war is still on, in case you haven't noticed." Misty's got a little too much attitude for me this morning. Whatever she, her mama, and Esmeralda are doing over there has given Misty a new confidence I don't like. Too bad Misty uses her powers for evil, even before she started wearing her blue contact lenses. And like Nellie's blond weave, the shit just looks wrong.

"What's that supposed to mean?" I ask my nemesis, who looks quite fierce in her tight-fitting jean dress and black heels. She doesn't have a sweater on with those short sleeves and should be cold, but maybe evil never chills. If I didn't have on my pretty pink North Face jacket Jeremy bought me for Christmas, I'd be an icicle by now.

"You'll see, Jayd. You'll see," Misty says, turning on her

heel and walking down the street toward Greenleaf, one of my alternate bus routes to Redondo Beach. I wonder why KJ didn't give her a ride to school. Something about Misty is bothering me more than usual, but I'll have to figure out that messy mystery later. I open the driver's door and place my backpack and purse in the backseat before sitting down and starting the car. I hope Bryan heard me, because I'm ready to roll.

"Have fun walking to the bus stop in those heels!" I yell after Misty. I've got to give it to the girl—she can strut. She can also be very vulgar with her hand gestures, but she doesn't scare me. I've already whipped her ass once, and as long as I've got my ancestors by my side, I can do it again if need be.

"Jayd, you ready?" Bryan asks, getting into the car, visibly relaxed from his usual morning spliff and completely unaware of the drama in my world. If we had time to talk this morning, I would spill my guts to my favorite uncle. But Bryan and I both have work to do and need to move fast if we're going to get anything done today.

~ 5 ~
Change Happens

"Yeah, I got some changin' to do."
—JOHN LEGEND

I don't even remember how I drove the forty-five minutes it takes me to get from Compton to Redondo Beach this morning in less than forty, but I'm here and ready to get on with my day. I wish I could call my mom from mind to mind like she does me, but I'll have to settle for using my cell later. It's not fair that her powers work in only one direction. Had my mom appreciated her powers when she was my age, there's no telling how dope her shit would have been. Now her gift of sight works to get into only my head, no one else's. I sure could use my mom's help this morning, but it'll have to wait until I see her tonight, if she comes home before going to her boyfriend's apartment for the weekend. She's a professional at arguing with her mother and eventually gets over it, whereas I, on the other hand, always feel bad after having a disagreement with Mama.

Mr. Adewale could tell something was up with me in first period. I wanted to talk to him about my issues, but because he has such a profound respect for Mama and our lineage, I doubt he'll take my side. What am I thinking, leaving Mama's house? But if I don't do something fast, I'm in danger of not passing my AP exams, and I'll be damned if I give Mrs. Bennett the satisfaction of seeing me fail. Besides, I've worked my ass off for two years on the AP track and deserve to study for my exams in peace.

The only good thing about this freaky Friday is that my mom's powers have been off the chain. The people I come into contact with all let me inside their minds with no idea of what I'm doing, and I can't help it—I can hear everything they're thinking. It's like verbal diarrhea in my head. And the fact that some of it is audible doesn't help keep the noise down, but it did help me chill out Nellie and Mickey for the time being. My mom's persuasive techniques can cool almost any situation and turn it to her advantage, I see. I've decided not to tell Mama or my mom about my newfound sight. I'm not ready to give up this power just yet.

"Hey, girl," Mickey says as she and Nellie approach my locker. They've been texting me all day about the baby shower this weekend, and I'm not any more excited about it than I was last week or the week before. I'll just be glad when it's all over. Mickey's still sour about Mrs. Esop inviting me to become a debutante, but I think Nigel has helped calm her down about the entire situation, especially since I agreed only for Mickey's sake. And Nellie hasn't said a word about dinner at Chance's house earlier this week. I heard what they wanted to say to me before I mentally resolved their issues during the pass between first and second period, and I am grateful I could squash that girl fight before it surfaced.

"Hey," I say unenthusiastically. Reid and Laura are passing out fliers for some Associated Student Body event I could not care less about. Nellie and her platinum hair are right on the back of the bandwagon with them. She tries to hand me a yellow paper, and I ignore the gesture. The last thing I need is another piece of trash in my locker. I think the environmental club should set up an official tribunal and put ASB on trial for unnecessarily killing trees to advertise their useless bull.

"What's got your panties all up in a bunch?" Nellie asks, reading the sour expression written all over my face while placing the paper back in the pile she's carrying. This morning's battle—not to mention the plastic-coated couch—left me feeling twisted.

"Just shit," I say, not wanting to relive the drama. "What's up with you?"

"Oh, bitch, you have to see the outfit I picked out for the shower. It's too cute." There Nellie goes with that word again. I guess Mickey's resolved not to fight it any further, but I'm denouncing the apparent brainwashing of which our girl's bleached hair is reflective.

"Nellie, I know you know my name," I say, slamming my locker door shut and facing the two of them while the rest of the crowded hall buzzes around us. I'm in no mood for her bougie ways.

"Bitch, please," Nellie says, not fully feeling my rage. "It's just a word, like I said before. You're going to be using it before you know it." She and Mickey lead us down the hall, but I'm stuck on Nellie's blatant disregard for my feelings. Has she completely lost her mind?

"All I know is if you call me that again, you better mean it and be ready to fight like a bitch." I know that was a bit harsh, but I've already told Nellie not to refer to me like that. There are so many other titles she could have chosen. Why that one stuck is a mystery to me. But who knows what Nellie's ever thinking. It's just like her and this blond phase. I can't wait to get my hands in her head and bring my girl back to center. I think she's more lost than I am right now, but she's afraid to admit it. If I weren't rushing to get to government class, I'd take the time to school Nellie.

"Jayd, calm down," Mickey says between bites of her Nacho Cheese Doritos. "We'll see you at lunch."

"No, you won't, because I have to study." When we cross the threshold leading from one opening in the main hall to the history hall, I can see Jeremy leaning up against the wall outside our third-period classroom. Noticing us walk in, Jeremy smiles my way, and I return the favor. He's exactly what I need to focus on for the rest of the day.

"What about at basketball practice this afternoon? We'll be there waiting for Nigel to get out." I wonder if Nellie still knows she sounds like one of Nigel's groupies instead of his baby-mama's best friend?

"Yeah, I guess so, but I don't have much time. I have to go to work," I say, reluctantly surrendering to my friends' collective will. The tension will be thick at work this afternoon, but at least it should be full of clients. That way, Mama and I can avoid each other and not get into it at the shop.

"Later, Jayd," Mickey and Nellie say, turning the corner at the end of the hall and leaving me to my man and our class. We'll see each other in speech and debate next period, where I'm sure the all-about-baby talk will continue. As Jeremy opens his arms for me to fall into his energetic embrace, I feel more grateful than ever to have him in my life. Where there's Jeremy, there's rational behavior. Maybe he can teach me how to change up my stylo and be as laid-back as he always seems to be, because this shit I'm dealing with is getting old, for real.

The rest of the school day was productive and just the distraction I needed from my personal bull. I left a message for my mom, giving her the full rundown of what happened with Mama and will fill in the rest of the details tonight. There was no dressing out in my weight-lifting class today, so I got to sit in the gym with my girls and watch the boys prep for the basketball game tonight as planned. I miss hanging out with my friends. All I ever seem to do is work, work, work, and the people I'm working with don't seem to appreciate my presence anymore. Ironically, I feel the same neglect in my current conversation with Nellie.

"Okay, so this is the shirt. I figured we'd go with a bright yellow because it's spring and it's a girl. It also sets off the yellow sparkles in the House of Deréon jeans we'll be wearing," she says, describing every detail of her outfit for the party on Sunday like she's going to be on the red carpet. Nellie has explained in full detail the importance of being both the hostesses and the godmothers at this baby shower, and the outfits must live up to our roles. She's also suggesting that we wear the same damn thing. What did they use in that hair dye?

"I like the gear, but I think we'll be all right if we don't match," I say, watching KJ, Nigel, Del, Money, Chance, and the opposing team smash each other on the court. They look ready to beat whichever team they're facing tonight.

"I wouldn't lie to you. It's how all the celebrity showers are being done now, and Nigel and Mickey's baby deserves the same thing. After all, Nigel's going to the NFL right out of college, so he's already a star." Mickey beams with pride as she watches her man hustle down the court. Nigel's dad wants him to focus on his basketball skills because he retired from the NBA. But Nigel lives for football season. "Bible, Jayd." And if Nellie says that Kardashian phrase to me one more time, I'm going to pick another good book out of my backpack to throw at her. But before I can reach complete annoyance with my girl, Rah rolls into the parking lot next to the gym. Damn. I should've known Rah would be here to see Nigel before the game tonight.

"Uh-oh," Mickey says, acknowledging Rah get out of his Acura and walk into the gymnasium. He spots us sitting on the sidelines and heads over.

"What's up, ladies?" Rah says. Mickey and Nellie say hey

and continue watching the game. "Jayd, can I holla at you outside for a minute? I want to apologize for the way I acted last Sunday."

"Is that even possible?" I ask, rising from the bleacher and following him outside. It's been overcast all day, threatening rain, but none has fallen. I hope it doesn't start when I get on the road in a few minutes. I hate driving in the rain.

"Jayd, come on. Can you blame me?" Rah asks, lowering his voice so the coaches and other players hanging outside don't hear him; neither one of us wants to make a scene around all these white folks. "You act like you don't know what this is. No matter how many dudes you go out with or how many girls I date, it's always going to be you and me."

"Whatever, Rah," I say, moving away from him, but he grabs my folded arms, pulling me into him. Damn, he smells good. Now his cologne is going to be all up in my nostrils for the rest of the day, bringing back nostalgia and shit.

"Whatever nothing," Rah says, attempting to hug me, but I wrestle free of his grasp. If he gets me entangled in those ripped ebony arms, I'll never keep my cool. "What's your problem?" He looks genuinely hurt, but I have to be strong in my stance.

"My problem is and has always been that you have many, many more girls than I do dudes. It's time to change shit up, Rah. I'm tired of your crap." A few of the players look in our direction, but we're being low-key even though the conversation is intense.

"But I'll always respect you as my queen." Like I give a damn about sharing his throne.

"No more buts, Rah. Your love of ass is what got us in this shit right now."

"So that's it—just like that, you're going back to the white boy?" Rah asks as Chance comes outside for some fresh air and a cigarette as if he could smoke on campus. If he were on the basketball team and not just taking it for his PE elective, I'm positive Chance would've quit smoking by now.

"What's up, my peeps?" Chance says, trying to lighten the mood. But there's no hope of us coming to any type of resolution today. Rah looks at Chance and nods before going inside. He can be mad all he wants, but Rah knows I'm right. If he weren't running around with fast girls, we would still be together. If anyone's to blame for the way we turned out, it's him.

Chance shrugs at me, takes out his iPod headphones, and puts them in his ears. I walk past him back into the building, and he's right behind me, bopping along to the music in his head. I guess he's done playing for today, and I'm done watching. The bell's about to ring, and I should leave early to beat the after-school crowd in the parking lot.

"Hey, Chance, can I see what's on your iPod? I need to upload mine with some new music," I say, taking the small electronic device from his hand and glancing at his playlist.

"You know you ain't gon' find what you're looking for in there. He don't get down like we do," Mickey says, making herself laugh, and she's the only one. I guess she'll never get tired of cracking on the white boy in our crew. Jeremy's much more of a rogue spirit and doesn't hang with us like Chance does now that he's dating Nellie.

"What makes you black, Mickey? I mean, for real," Nellie says, looking sideways at her man. "Some of the white people we go to school with know more about black culture than some of the black people I know."

"The answer to that question lies in your zip code, Nellie. Or have you forgotten you live only five minutes away from me in Compton?" Mickey's thinking is so limited it's sad. Nigel's mom will never find that shit tolerable. I have faith that Mickey can change and grow, but I doubt Mrs. Esop sees Mickey the same way I do.

"Being black is about more than where I live, Mickey," Nellie says, rolling her eyes. "I know I'm black and beautiful, isn't that right, baby?" I notice she didn't mention anything about her loving her black hair, but I'm going to leave that topic alone for right now. I know Nellie's sensitive about her shit.

"You're damn right," Chance says, kissing Nellie on the neck and making us all sick.

"Even if Chance lived in our hood, he would still be the little white boy he is, no matter how he dresses or what kind of car he drives, no offense," Mickey says, but I think there's plenty of offense taken. Rah turns around from where he's posted up on the wall and shakes his head at our conversation. He agrees with Mickey but on a completely different level. I would, too, but there's one important missing link that would squash this entire debate.

"What if I told you you were black, too?" I ask Chance, who looks like he's had the wind knocked out of him. The bell rings, suspending the question in the air. My girls rise from our bleacher, and Rah follows them to center court, where Nigel's still shooting practice hoops, leaving Chance and I to talk one-on-one.

"Jayd, why do you keep saying that?" Chance asks. I look into his hazel eyes and see his questions clearly. He knows he's got black in his blood but can't explain it.

"What if it was true?"

Chance looks down at his latest Jordans, basketball shorts, and expensive watch. He's sizing himself up against his dad, against Jeremy.

"I don't know," Chance says, mulling the idea over in his head for himself. "I guess it would explain a lot." I guess he really doesn't know his birth story after all, and if I stay in his head too long, I might accidentally tell him, and that's not my place. Luckily, I can jump out of a mind even if I can't control when I'm going to jump in.

"Maybe you should talk to your parents about it." I grab my backpack and purse off the bleacher beside me and stand up, ready to get out of here. Work calls, and so does my money.

"Oh, I don't think that's a good idea. If my dad found out I had an ounce of black blood, he'd probably jump off the roof out of shame." I almost wish that were true, but I already know Mr. Carmichael knows about Chance's birth parents, and he's still standing.

"What about your mom?" I glance across the court at Rah, Nigel, and my girls, wishing everything could be back to normal for us. Rah glares at me before refocusing on his conversation.

"My mom's cool. She's real supportive of me finding myself. She's always talking about the world being my oyster and crazy shit like that. She's kind of out there." Chance smiles and looks down at his watch, thinking of his mom. Part of his struggle with questioning his mother is that he doesn't want to cause her any more pain. He hates the way his father treats her and does his best not to add to her misery.

"Maybe she's not as out there as you think she is." I look deep into Chance's eyes, praying for some recognition of the fact that his parents adopted him and that his birth mother is half black, but I've got nothing. Mama said my memory is a gift, so should I share my blessing with him or not?

"So, what's up with you and that new sophomore Emilio?" Chance asks, officially changing the subject. "You got that freshman fever a year after the fact, huh?" Chance rises from his seat next to mine, and we walk outside as the final school bell rings. I'd better wrap up this conversation and get to hiking up the hill to my car. Besides, if Nellie comes out here and finds me still rapping with her man, she'll bust a vein, no matter how innocent the conversation may be.

"Nothing. I know you know Jeremy and I are back together,

so don't even play like that." I reach up and push Chance on the shoulder, slightly knocking his tall, thin frame off balance and into his car.

"I'll never understand why you drive this old thing," Nellie says, following us outside and interrupting our conversation while tossing the catalogs and other crap she's holding into Chance's open car window.

"Nellie, what do you mean? This here is a 1967 Chevy Nova, baby girl. It's one of the fastest hot rods around," Chance says, pushing a button on his hi-tech car remote and turning on the stereo. He is so proud of his boy toy, but Nellie's not feeling the love.

"I know you can afford something better than this," Nellie says, flipping her golden locks over her right shoulder. That habit of hers got on my nerves with her naturally brown hair, and it's even more annoying now. "Don't you miss the luxuries of a new car?" That sure is a lot of lip coming from someone who doesn't drive.

"Baby, that's not me. This is how I roll," Chance says, turning up the bass in his already loud sounds. Nigel, Mickey, and Rah, who are now behind us, look impressed with the Gucci Mane song bumping from his speakers. And Mickey thought he didn't have the type of music we like. She's the main one rocking back and forth, and her baby is probably in her belly dancing, too.

"It just looks so . . . so . . ." Nellie says, pausing for effect, I suppose.

"So what?" I ask, already knowing what she's thinking without reading her mind. Nellie's the kind of neighbor who will call the police on your ass in a hot minute if your music's too loud rather than simply ask you to turn it down if it's that serious. She's also the type of Compton native who hates being from there. And Chance is the type of white boy who would love a shot at being from our hood. I'm still torn about telling him he's part black, but the truth just might make his day. Change is an inevitable part of life, as I'm learning. Eventually, my boy's going to have to learn about his heritage.

"So Mexican." We all pause and wait for Nellie to laugh so we can know that what she just said was a joke, but the laughter never comes.

"What's wrong with that?" Chance asks, putting Nellie on the spot. She looks embarrassed, as well she should, because she's gone too far this time. I guess my morning mouthing-off illness is contagious.

"I love your car," I say. Nigel and Rah smile at me as I touch the red hood like we're good friends. "Can I drive her up to the main lot?" I ask, redirecting Chance's attention the old-fashioned way because I can't jump in anyone's head right now. I have to get to work and could use a ride to my car.

"Sure," he says, opening the driver's-side door for me before getting in the passenger's side. I wave bye to my friends and turn the key, feeling the quiet purr of the engine surge up my right leg. I press on the gas while in park and then the brake before putting the classic car into reverse. I love driving this thing.

"That's it, Jayd. Nice and easy," Chance says, smiling at the sight of me behind the wheel of his winning ride. Whoever worked on this Nova didn't leave anything out. The vibrating bass, leather seats, and fresh air are so therapeutic for my soul. Too bad I can't drive it all the way to Compton. I need to stay in this moment for as long as I can before encountering Mama. I admit it will be difficult moving out of Mama's house, but it'll be worth it in the end. Like all change, it's coming whether we like it or not. I'm always moving too fast for my own good, so I'll just cruise into the eye of the tornado this afternoon and enjoy the calm before the storm that is Mama.

~ 6 ~
Greener Pastures

*"I need a roof over my head /
And bread on my table."*

—Sugar Minott

After taking my time getting to my mom's car, I finally make my way to Netta's shop. I'm apprehensive about seeing Mama after this morning's quarrel but equally ready to get it over with. When Netta buzzes me through the front door, the conversation is in full swing. I greet everyone, and they continue their discussion. With the four clients present, I'm sure it's been a lively chat. I walk to the back of the shop and put my purse in my locker, claim my personalized apron, and get ready to work.

"I don't know why black women are so fascinated with James Bond, no matter which white man is playing him." Netta's in rare form this afternoon. "Did you see that movie *Live and Let Die* where they demonized a voodoo priest? Like they couldn't pick something else to talk about. No, they just had to go feeding my black men to some damn sharks as if we didn't get enough of that bull during the Middle Passage," Netta says, clamping the hot curlers like they wrote the script. Poor curlers and client at her booth.

"Mmmm-hmmm," Mama says. That's the most she's said—or not said—since I arrived. Mama hasn't said one word to me directly, and she barely looked my way when I walked in. I know Netta's trying to break the ice, but it's colder than

Alaska in here, and I don't feel a warm front coming on anytime soon, especially not after I break the news to Mama that
I actually am moving into my mom's place and speaking at
Daddy's church for the unholy day. It's like two betrayals in
one shot, or at least that's the way she'll see it, knowing
Mama. She and Rah have that whole loyalty-to-the-end personality streak in common.

I step into Netta's private bathroom and wash my hands
and face in the sink before I officially start my duties. I quickly
stop in the shrine room and say my prayers before going
back out front, where the topic has progressed to Halle Berry's
role as a Bond girl in one of the movies. I could not care less
about all that. On my way to the clients' cabinets, I look
across the room at Mama, who looks preoccupied with her
own thoughts—probably about me. There's no time like the
present to break the news to her, but I'll wait until the clients
leave. The shop will be empty soon enough, leaving us space
and time to talk in private.

Once the shop is quiet, Netta and Mama recap the day's
events, mostly about which clients' hair is growing stronger
and who needs what in her personal beauty regime. I've been
replaying my independence speech in my head for the past
four hours, trying to figure out which words go where, and
have come to the conclusion that I should just let them flow.
Here goes nothing. We're all busy washing the various tools
necessary for our trade. Hopefully, the water will keep us all
mellow when I break the news.

"Daddy wants me to give the young folks' sermon on
Easter Sunday," I say as Mama washes the combs in the small
sink. "I told him I'd think about it." Netta looks up at me
from her sink and returns her attention to the brushes she's
soaking. I guess she doesn't want to get in the middle of this
discussion.

"I'm sure you will," Mama says, taking the handful of multi-colored plastic hair combs out of the soapy water and putting them on the empty side of the sink for me to rinse. I walk over to where she's standing and begin my duties. "Do you know why he asked you to speak?" Mama continues washing, and I continue rinsing as I think of a response. Even though her eyes are looking down, I can still feel her probing my thoughts the same as if she were looking directly into my eyes.

"Not really," I say while laying the combs on a clean white towel to dry. "I guess he thought I did a good job at Tre's memorial service a few weeks ago. He seemed proud of the way I stood up in front of everyone and poured the libation for the ancestors." Mama washes the last of the combs and passes them to me before rinsing out the sink. She takes one of the white towels hanging from the cabinet above our heads and dries her hands.

"I'm not doubting your grandfather's pride in your speaking abilities, Jayd. But I would be doing you a disservice if I didn't warn you about his need to save the poor sinner's soul," Mama says, taking the clients' boxes out of the same cabinet to reorganize their contents. Netta's now doing the same thing with boxes in the cabinet above her sink. We're nothing if not thorough at Netta's salon.

"Mama, Daddy knows I don't need saving." As I put the last comb on the towel to dry, Mama looks at my every movement carefully, like she's measuring me up. I turn around, retrieving the same towel she used, to dry my hands before checking the wall clock. My mom still hasn't called me back yet, but I'm sure she got my message. If it's all good with her, I can move my stuff tonight.

"Does he really?" Mama's deep inhalation sounds heavy, like she's breathing for more than herself. The memory she's processing must be serious by the way she's choosing her words carefully.

"Mmmm-hmmm," Netta says while tagging the various boxes with a list of needed ingredients. I know she wants to comment, but she refrains. Mama looks at me and shakes her head, taking her time responding. Finished with my duties in the wash area, I move back into the main area, awaiting my next assignment. Waiting for Mama to speak, I pick up the salt and pepper shakers sitting on the small table next to the hair driers and begin to spin them around like I used to do when I was a child. We need to refill the other condiments and napkins for the clients who like to munch while getting their hair done. Mama and Netta usually provide them with something good to snack on to pass the time.

"Do you know why we throw salt over our shoulders when we spill it?" Mama asks and then walks over to where I'm standing, claiming the shakers and my attention.

Without waiting for my answer, Mama continues.

"It's for the ancestors. Everything we do is because of the ones who came before us—no exceptions. I'm all for people hearing God the way It comes to them. But as I've said before, the moment when that hearing comes with judgment, it becomes not only dangerous but also disrespectful for those deemed as nonbelievers. And trust me, your grandfather thinks of you as a nonbeliever—someone who needs saving. The day I meet a Christian who doesn't look at me like I'm already burning in hell, with little devils poking me in my backside with pitchforks, will be the day that I set foot back in a church." I know what she means. When I told my class I come from a lineage of voodoo priestesses, I felt the heat in their imaginations rise under my chair.

"But I don't understand how he could, especially after he's seen the work we do." Mama looks at me, smiling at my naïveté. "Besides, he wouldn't ask me to give the sermon if he thinks I'm going to hell." I quickly restock the necessities and dust the table and magazines. I know once I move out of this conversation and into the next one about me moving out, it'll be time to go, in more ways than one.

"He would if he thought it might save your soul." Mama returns to the wash area, reaches into the cabinet above Netta's head, and claims Netta's spirit book. Walking back over to the table, she sets the heavy book down and turns to a section on sacrifice.

"I know you think I'm being naive about this, but I honestly think Daddy's coming around a bit," I say, directing my attention to where her red-tipped fingernail is pointing. Mama looks up from the worn pages just long enough to roll her emerald eyes at me before she continues her searching. I wonder what she's looking for? We should get to work on an index for this massive book. Much like ours, Netta's is in need of some serious updating.

"I know you want to believe in the good in everyone, and that's what makes you so sweet, omo Oshune," Mama says, stroking my left cheek while calling me a child in Yoruba. At least I know she still loves me no matter how hurt she is by my recent actions. "But as a daughter of Oshune, you have to also be aware of when your culture is under attack. That is also part of Oshune's character—to keep our culture alive. And trust me, child, your grandfather is not interested in the retention of traditional African religion, no matter what you may think his true motives are."

Without saying another word, Mama taps her long, French-manicured nail on a page for me to begin this evening's studies. It's one of her own stories that Netta recorded. She returns to her work and leaves me to my reading. I can understand Mama's caution, but I think she's overreacting on this one. Nothing about Daddy's invitation said to me "save the sinner," but we shall see. I don't even know if I want to go through with it. I don't mind speaking in front of a crowd, but Daddy's congregation is a whole other story.

"Diva is a female version of a hustler," Beyoncé sings, announcing a call. It's Jeremy. I told him all about this morning's drama, and he's been trying to catch up with me ever since. He'll be the first call I make when I leave work in a few minutes. Mama and Netta have a lot of work to do for the initiation they're helping with, as well as behind-the-scenes work for the shop, neither of which I'm privy to. After I'm done with the impromptu spirit lesson, I close the book, awaiting the customary drill from the two elders in the room, but it looks like something else is on Mama's mind.

"Your mother called me this afternoon to talk about your move," Mama says without looking at me. I can hear the tears in her voice, but neither one of us will let a tear drop. Stubbornness is in our genes. "Are you sure you want to do this?"

Netta looks up at me from her work with a concerned look in her eyes. I know they mean well, but I can't deal with my uncles and their rude-ass behavior any longer, nor should I have to if there's a better option available.

"Mama, I have exams this month that could make the difference between me getting into a good college or not getting in at all," I say, hanging my work apron on the hook next to the large cabinets taking up one side of the room. "I'm not leaving because I want to. I'm leaving because I need space to concentrate on my schoolwork." I glance at the clock and feel suddenly rushed for time with the looming lateness. It's almost eight, and I need to call Jeremy back before he goes night surfing with his beach crew.

"And what about your spirit work? How are you going to study if you're not at home with me?"

"With us," Netta says, now beating the shea butter she's mixing harder than necessary.

"Mama, you act like I'm not going to see you every day," I say, taking my purse out of the locker, ready to go. "And besides, just because I don't live with you and Daddy anymore doesn't mean I won't be back to visit." I dip my finger into the sweet butter Netta's making, to moisturize my hands.

"There's a reason you don't live with your mama, Jayd. First of all, she's never home, and you're still a minor. You need supervision." Mama's not going to let up on this, and I don't want to argue anymore. I wish I could jump in her mind and chill her out, but my mom's powers are not easy to master. How can I get Mama to understand that I deserve a break?

"Mama, I'm not a little girl anymore. I can take care of my-self. I've been doing a good job so far." I look at Mama and Netta, who look equally shocked by my statement, but it's true, and they can't argue with the facts. No one makes me do my schoolwork, buys my supplies or my clothes. That shit's all on me, and because of that, I should at least be able to study in peace.

"Jayd, please. Your grandfather and I provide for you, and your mother helps out when she can, or have you forgotten about groceries and bills?" Mama asks, reading my mind. I didn't think about the fact that my mom doesn't even keep the refrigerator stocked for me on the weekends, and I doubt she'll kick in for my weekday meals, especially because she's not there. Karl provides all her meals now. I'll make do on milk and cereal, if need be. It'll be worth it to have my own space.

"I'll be all right, Mama. Don't worry," I say, taking my keys out of my purse and making my way toward the front door. I would kiss them both good-bye, but I don't think they're in the mood for any affection. "I'd better get going before it gets too late."

"You're moving too fast, Jayd. But you'll soon learn your lesson." Mama sounds like Daddy, who always says I'm mov-ing so fast that no grass can grow underneath me. I don't know what that means, but it must be old folks' way of saying

I need to slow my ass down. But this time I disagree with them both. If they knew what my friends were up to all the time, they'd count their blessings that I move the way I do. Speaking of which, I guess I'd better get going if I'm going to move my stuff out of Daddy's closet and make my move official. There's no time like the present to see how green the grass is on my mom's side of town.

"I'll see y'all tomorrow," I say, waving to them as I close the door behind me. I feel like I'm doing the right thing, and, hopefully, they'll grow to understand my decision.

Earlier, I sent Jeremy a brief text saying to call me when he gets home tonight, no matter how late it is. I also texted Nigel and asked him to meet me at my mom's apartment and help me move my shit upstairs if he's not too tired from playing ball. I don't have a lot of stuff, but it's heavier than I thought it would be. Luckily, it's Friday night, and the house is empty. I take this as a good sign that I'm moving in the right direction, even if I am whipped from packing my belongings into the car.

I stack the last of my things in the dining room, ready to load them into my mom's car parked in the driveway. Daddy pulls up, parking in front of the house and walking up beside my mom's car and onto the porch steps.

"Hey, Daddy," I say, passing him by as I carry my things out.

"Hey, Tweet," he says, kissing me on the forehead as he eyes my actions. "Jayd, can I talk to you for a minute?" Daddy takes my bags and helps me to the car. I'm glad Mama's not here. I don't think I could handle moving while she's watching. It's bad enough I'm causing her so much pain, but, even worse, I wouldn't want her to see that me staying here would be painful for me. I hope she understands I'm not doing this to spite her, even if it feels that way.

"Yeah, Daddy. What's up?" I ask, stuffing the oversize black garbage bags into my mom's small car.

"What's up is you moving to your mama's house when you know it's not in your best interest. Your place is here, Tweet, and you know it."

"Daddy, it's just time." I close the trunk and then the passenger's door, ready to hit the road. I was excited until my grandfather came home. Although I'm grateful for Daddy's help, I don't need another guilt trip.

"Just be careful, Jayd. Sometimes we get more than we bargain for, even if we think it's the answer to our prayers." Daddy hugs me tightly and then goes inside the house, closing the door behind him. I get in the car, press the clutch, and start the engine, finally leaving Mama's house. I still can't believe I'm moving out, but the packed car is a reality check. There's no going back now, nor do I want to.

"So you're really moving out of Mama's house for good?" Nigel asks, helping me take the last of the Hefty bags out of the backseat. I put all my small things in two large Macy's shopping bags in the front passenger's side. I had no idea how much this Protegé could hold, but I have to say, I got all my belongings moved in one trip, and with Nigel and Rah helping me get everything up the stairs, it hasn't been that bad. I had to pick up Nigel and Rah from Rah's house because they were working on Nigel's ride. Sandy borrowed Rah's ride again without asking, and Nellie and Mickey went to get a pedicure and plan on meeting us back at Rah's house afterward.

"I don't know about all that, but right now I need my space," I say, pushing the last bag against the living room wall. I'll sort out all my shit later. Right now I need to get something in my stomach. I haven't eaten since lunch, and all this moving has made me hungry.

"Space for what?" Rah asks, bitter as ever. We're still barely speaking, but even when he's pissed at me, I know he'll come when I need him, even if I didn't ask him personally. Whether I like it or not, Nigel's always going to keep Rah up-to-date with my life. "It's not like you do anything but read and sleep anyway, unless the white boy has changed your usual routine."

"Excuse me?" I ask with my hands on my hips, ready to defend my relationship with Jeremy against this fool. He's got it twisted if he thinks I'm going to let him belittle me and my man's vibe.

"Okay, you two," Nigel says, lifting up his Adidas T-shirt and wiping the sweat from his brow. "We managed to get through an hour of moving peacefully. Can we keep it like that, or do I have to send you to your separate corners?" Rah glares at me, and we both decide to chill out for the time being. I know he's jealous, but damn. Green is not a good color on him.

"Thanks, you guys, for helping me out. I know you must be tired from the game tonight," I say, eyeing the work ahead of me. You'd think with all the moving I've done in my life that I'd be used to packing and unpacking by now, but I truly hate the process. I've always wished for my own permanent space, but until then, my mother's living room will have to do.

"It's no problem, Jayd. You know you're our girl," Nigel says, hugging me tight. Rah looks like he wants a hug, too, but doesn't budge from his angry stance.

"I'll meet y'all downstairs," Rah says, rolling his eyes at Nigel's affection for me. He's always so damn territorial, which is ironic because he belongs to no one.

"Let me treat y'all to some In-N-Out or something," I offer, grabbing my purse off the coatrack by the front door. I don't want to waste all my hard-earned money on fast food, but I have to repay them somehow. I'll go grocery shopping tomorrow and stock up on food for the week ahead.

"You don't need to pay us, girl. You know that," Nigel says.

"I know that, but I can feed my boys, can't I?" Nigel looks like he wants to protest but doesn't, and I'm thankful. As much as they've done for me, it feels good to be able to treat them for a change, no matter how much of an ass Rah's being tonight.

"Thank you," Nigel says, walking down the stairs ahead of me and toward the carport so I can lock up. When I make it to the car, Rah's blowing his steam off by smoking in my mom's ride. Oh no, he didn't.

"Hey, man, let me hit that," Nigel says upon entering vehicle, but they're both in for a rude awakening.

"Oh no, y'all don't," I say, getting in and starting the engine. "There will be no weed smoking up in here."

"Are you serious?" Nigel says, hitting the blunt before passing it back to an already faded Rah.

"Hell yeah, I'm serious if for no other reason than this isn't my car. My mom doesn't condone smoking anything in her house or car; you know that," I say, buckling my seat belt. "Not to mention the fact that we're minors, it's illegal, and I don't want my hair smelling like an ashtray. Now put it out and roll down the windows to let some fresh air in." They both smile at me and respect my wishes. "Thank you. I know y'all can wait until you get home for that shit."

"Sure thing, Miss Jackson," Nigel says, smiling at my vehemence. I shift the gear into reverse and get a move on, ready to grub.

"No offense," Rah says, and I know he didn't mean any. Everyone else might be cool with smoking in the car, but I'm not. I don't get why black men would want to give the cops another reason to stop them and lock their asses up when being black while driving is reason enough. My uncle Bryan smokes in his van all the time and anywhere else he can. I'm just waiting for us to get a phone call to come bail his ass out of the county jail. My other uncles are regular residents already, for possession and other petty shit they're constantly getting picked up on. I know most teenagers would go buck wild if they moved into their own place, which is basically what living with mom will be like, but this ain't that type of party. And the sooner I lay down the law, the better.

~ 7 ~

Birthday Bequest

*"That little glimpse of light /
Makes that diamond really shine."*

—BEYONCÉ

After slamming down a cheeseburger, fries, and chocolate shake, I'm ready to go home and chill. When Nigel called to see if Mickey had eaten, she and Nellie were still caught up getting everything waxed and whatnot. It's close to ten, and rather than wait for them to show up at Rah's, I decided to head back to my mom's and call it a night. As usual, Friday night is lively on Larch Street, with so many cars parked on the tight block there's barely any room to drive. Luckily, I don't have to park my mom's car on the street, now that she spends all her free time at Karl's place. I don't remember the last time she spent a night in her own bed. If she keeps it up, I'm going to change the sheets and make it my own. I have a busy workday ahead of me tomorrow, and it's nights like these I could use a good sleep in an actual bed instead of on the couch.

As I approach the top of the stairs, I hear someone in the apartment. I hope it's my mom because I don't feel like fighting off an intruder this evening. My friends can really suck the energy out of me. I unlock the door with my pepper-spray key chain ready to spray, just in case.

"Hey, Mom," I say, thankful it's her. I walk into the crowded living room and lock the door behind me. She kisses me on the cheek, noticing my most recent gift from Jeremy.

"Where did you get this from?" she asks, picking up the small cloth doll off the couch and eyeing it carefully. I guess she's looking for pins, but we don't fix voodoo dolls—anymore. Mama says that's not our style, and I'm glad for it. The last thing I want is a bunch of tortured-looking dolls all over the place, but this one is too cute.

"Jeremy gave it to me as a peace offering after he found out I was a priestess," I say, wiping off the living room table before moving some of my stuff from the couch. It's been a while since anyone dusted up in here. My mom has never been much of a homemaker and doesn't apologize for it either. I hope Karl knows what he's getting into, now that they're engaged.

"Oh my," she says, fingering the miniature yellow-and-white-checkered dress. "I used to have a doll like this on my shrine." I can't imagine my mother ever having a shrine. She has trinkets here and there that are reminiscent of the religion, but no sacred space for the ancestors or orishas. Maybe I should change that because I'm going to be spending more time here.

"Oh no, you don't," my mom says, responding aloud to my thought. "There are no shrines up in here. What if Karl comes in and sees them? I want to get the other ring on my finger before we go there," my mom says, eyeing her emerald and diamond engagement ring before heading to her room to pack and unpack. "And all your shit needs to be out of my living room. You'll have to make space for it somewhere else, Jayd."

"How about your closet and dresser? It's not like you're here all that much anyway," I say, eyeing her messy room as I follow her inside. She's got designer clothes strewn across the bed and dirty laundry piled on the floor. The only time she comes home is when she needs to replenish her wardrobe, and I've noticed that certain things are missing. I think she's slowly but surely moving in with her fiancé, and I'm sure that's fine with him. Karl is sprung.

"True, but I'm not giving up my space just yet, little one. But I'll tell you what—you can have one drawer and some space at the back of the closet. That's where all my big-girl clothes are, and I don't plan on using them anytime soon. Although, if my man keeps taking me to all these good restaurants, I'm going to need them." I hear that. Jeremy feeds me like a soon-to-be-roasted pig, too, and I love him for it.

"Thank you," I say, walking over to the closet and pushing the hangers aside. I have a lot of work ahead of me. Good thing I came home early enough to get it done and can hopefully still get to bed early enough for some good sleep.

"You're welcome, but you know the grass ain't greener over here, Miss Jackson. Just because Mama ain't here doesn't mean you can get your party on. You'll have to buy your own groceries and keep the house clean," she says. I don't see what's changing. I've always had to do those things.

"Okay," I say, sorting through her supposed big-girl gear. It's only two sizes from where she is now. I can probably fit most of this stuff now and will surely try them on to see before moving them out. It's going to be great living here. Not only will I have peace from all my uncles, but I will also have my mom's wardrobe at my disposal on a daily basis. Happy birthday to me, for real. "So what's up for our birthday?" I ask, already knowing she and Mama have plans for us like they do every year.

"Well, this year I've got my man to celebrate with. He's an Aries, too, you know," she says from the hallway where she's collecting toiletries from the hall closet. I miss watching my mom's beauty rituals.

"No, I didn't know, but that's cool. Is he coming with us?"

My mom looks at me, and I already know there's no "us" this year. "Mama's going to have a fit if we don't celebrate with her."

"I know, but she loves Karl. Hopefully, she won't be too pissed, not that your premature departure has helped any." Now that's a low blow.

"Mom, she doesn't love Karl that much. Do you know Mama at all?" I ask. She can be unbelievable sometimes. I don't enjoy sharing my birthday with her every year, but what choice do I have, really?

You always have a choice, Jayd, my mom says to me, her mind to mine. She places her nail polish, cotton balls, and other necessities in the side pocket of her duffel bag and zips it closed. I hope she can't tell that I've retained some of her old powers from my dream last night.

"Why are you talking to me telepathically when you're right in front of me?" I ask, watching my mom hurriedly stuff her belongings into the brown bag, ready to return to her second home. And Daddy thinks I'm the one moving too fast.

Because I want you to feel me, Jayd. You're going to be seventeen next week, and I'm going to be twenty-five again, she says, eleven years shy of her real age. But no one would guess my mom's in her midthirties. *It's time we cut the cord and celebrate both our days individually, don't you think?*

"I feel you, but you know how Mama feels about traditions." I eye the flyy Prada shoes my mom kicks off and replaces with a pair of red Gucci stilettos, providing the perfect accent to her long black dress. With her ebony hair hanging down her back and green eyes blinging like the expensive rock on her ring finger, my mom's quite a sight to behold.

"Maybe we can start a new tradition, like brunch for our birthdays or something like that," she says, checking her reflection in the closet mirror one last time. I guess she and Karl have planned a night out.

"Yeah, maybe, if Mama lets us live that long." I follow my mom back into the living room. She's packed and ready to go. I guess she'll do her laundry another time. Before she leaves for the evening, my mom takes a small gold box out of her purse on the coffee table and hands it to me.

"Happy early birthday, baby," my mom says, passing me the tiny box. Good things come in small packages. I tear into the gold wrapping, anxious for my surprise.

"My birthday's not until Wednesday, mom," I say, taking out the tissue paper disguising my gift. Is it a new pair of earrings or maybe a ring? I open the package and find a thin black box inside.

"It's gold, but not for you to wear. I know it's not what you were expecting, but I thought it's the best gift a mother could give her daughter on her seventeenth birthday."

"Condoms!?" I ask, shouting more than inquiring. "You bought me condoms for my birthday!?" I can't believe my mom sometimes, and now is definitely one of those times.

"Yes, little Miss Thang," she says, zipping her Louis Vuitton duffel bag and suitcase before grabbing her purse and sweater from the coatrack. "Better safe than sorry. Ask your little friend Mickey. I'm sure she'll tell you the same thing." She doesn't know Mickey very well, because in her world, Mickey's won the lotto by being pregnant and claiming Nigel as the daddy. Even if he doesn't go to the NFL, his family is loaded, and that's all Mickey needs—no prophylactics included.

"Mom, I don't need these," I say, returning the condoms to their box, tissue paper and all. "That's all you got me for my birthday?"

"Like you said, your birthday's not until Wednesday, and depending on what I get for mine the day before, we'll see what else you get from me," she says, smiling and kissing me on my cheek before ducking out. Even though it may sound selfish, she's actually hooking me up. Her men always give the best gifts, and she usually gets a shopping trip out of it, too. And that's where my bonus gifts come from.

"Be careful, Mom, and I love you," I say after her. My mom's a lot to handle on a good day. I hope Karl's ready for the trip.

"Ditto," she says from the bottom of the stairs. I lock the multiple bolts and chains on the front door and look at the mess I've made moving. I'd better get to work organizing this space if I'm going to make it to bed at a decent time. Tomorrow morning will be here before I know it, not to mention Mickey's shower on Sunday. I still haven't picked out an outfit for the backyard boogie at Nigel's house. I know my mom's closet can help me in that department, but I'll worry about that later. Right now I just need to make it to work tomorrow.

After my mom left last night, I claimed my space, took a hot steam bath, and went straight to bed. I hardly ever get to take baths uninterrupted at Mama's house. Now that I'm here, I think I'll take one every night just because I can. And I know whose ass has been in it, so there's no need to bleach down the tub every time before I get in. Mama says steam does wonders for our skin, and I believe her. When I take a hot bath without anything in it, my skin feels soft and smooth. And when we add Mama's magical ingredients for everything we can think of, everything feels fresh and clean and new, just like a head cleansing.

I got up early this morning, did Shawntrese's hair—which is luminous, thanks to Mama's magical hair line and my own skills—and headed straight to Netta's and worked all day long. Mama barely talked to me, and I was glad for it. All we ever seem to do nowadays is argue, and it was too busy a day for negative energy. I raked up almost a hundred dollars in tips and am due a birthday gift for myself. It'll have to wait until the actual day, and that's fine with me. Maybe by Wednesday I'll have a few more birthday bucks under my belt, and then I can really do some damage at the mall.

Jeremy and I finally got a chance to catch up this afternoon. He was very sympathetic, but I know he can't imagine what I'm going through, moving out of Mama's house. It's just like when I told Nellie and Mickey about it when we talked last night—their whole point was that I should've been living with my mother in the first place. No one understands how close Mama and I are or how painful this is for us both, but Jeremy did send me a text with a picture of a dozen roses attached. At least he's making an effort to feel me.

Jeremy and I also made plans to celebrate my birthday tonight. It's not a party like I wanted, but I'm sure I'll have just as much fun hanging out with my boo. I didn't have time to go grocery shopping like I'd planned. I have to shop for Mickey's party tomorrow anyway, so I'll have to get my food then, too.

As usual, Jeremy's right on time. I got home less than two hours ago and managed to do my hair, pick out a casual, yet sexy outfit from my mom's closet, and get a little studying done. I had a chance to look through my mom's spirit notebook and found out that when her powers were first developing, she didn't have any control over when she could use them, much like I'm experiencing with her powers and my own ability to jump in and out of my dreams. I'm going to have to put a lot of thought into controlling my sight if I plan on getting better at using my gifts. Once the AP exams are over, I'll have more time to focus on my personal prowess as a priestess. Right now I just want to enjoy being a fierce sistah who has a fine-ass boyfriend ready to take her out for a much needed night on the town.

"Come on in, Mr. Weiner," I say, opening the door and stepping aside so Jeremy can get the full effect of my appearance. Jeremy moves behind me, reaching his arm high above my head and pushing the door shut. He then turns me around to face him, forcing my back up against the door. I have nowhere to go, nor do I want to move. He's wearing a different cologne tonight but smells as good as ever.

"You look nice," he says, bending down and whispering into my ear. His breath is warm as he brushes his soft lips against the side of my neck. "And you taste even better." I close my eyes and let him take over. We're in no rush.

"Is that right?" I inquire, barely audible. I lose all thought and reason once Jeremy and I get started. I stretch myself up to meet Jeremy's lips, giving him a proper kiss hello. After several minutes of making out, we come up for air.

"Don't we have reservations somewhere or something?" I ask between pecks. I don't want to stop, but we'd better go before we find use for my mother's odd birthday gift. Even if she meant well, I still can't believe she bought me condoms.

"Actually, we don't. I was thinking we can take a ride to Malibu, but it's up to you. But we do have one stop to make first, if the lady doesn't mind." Jeremy smiles at me, his blue eyes shining in the living room light. It's the first day of spring, and love is definitely in the night air for me—and so is the chill. It's been cold and threatening to rain all week. Instead of my everyday jacket, I opt to wear one of my mother's warm wraps. The bright orange fabric goes well with my yellow dress, which is also compliments of my mom's closet.

"Not at all, especially if you're driving," I say, mistakenly thinking we're ready to leave, but apparently we're not done yet. Jeremy and I kiss for a few more minutes before finally heading out the door.

"So what do you want to do tonight? It's all about my girl and her special day," Jeremy says, placing his right hand on my left thigh as he guns the engine in his timeless Mustang, exciting me in more ways than one.

"Well, in that case, let's go to dinner. All I had to eat was some microwave popcorn at work today, and it was a long day." I spent ten hours on my feet today, with a short break between braiding and working at Netta's. I'm ready to relax.

"Your wish is my command," Jeremy says, pulling away from the curb and leading the way to a perfect evening. I don't care where we end up, as long as we arrive together.

Between the clouds are clearings revealing the dark night sky, providing a pleasant backdrop to our cruise. As usual, Sepulveda Boulevard is packed. There's never a time when the streets of Los Angeles are carless. Instead of making the left onto Pico Boulevard, which would take us toward the ocean, Jeremy makes a right. I thought we were going to Malibu, but he did say we had to make a stop first. Rather than question his navigation of the West LA area, I sit quietly and enjoy the ride.

"The Century City mall? What are we doing here?" I ask as we pull into the busy parking structure. He parks the car and turns off the engine.

"Not only does it have movies, it also has plenty of shopping," Jeremy says, handing me a platinum credit card with his name on it. "Happy birthday, Lady J. Tonight the mall is yours." I don't believe it. I feel like I'm living in my mother's world, not my own.

"Are you serious?" I inspect the card carefully, and it looks real enough to me. I've only seen the one Karl gave to my mom for Christmas. Brothahs in my hood are cash-only kinds of consumers. It's rare to find anyone with good credit, let alone a credit card with a high limit like this one.

"Am I Jeremy Weiner tonight?" I ask, stepping out of the door Jeremy's holding open for me. I glance around the huge structure and see that most of the luxury cars coming in are heading straight for the valet. There's not a hooptie in sight.

"No, but you are his girlfriend, and that's the next best thing."

I playfully sock Jeremy in the arm as he locks the car behind us. He can be so full of himself sometimes, and I love him for it.

"I wanted to get you a gift, but I didn't want you to think I was trying to buy you again or anything like that. Besides, I thought picking out your own gift would be more fun. I like to watch my woman shop," he says, putting his arm around my shoulders and kissing my forehead.

"I can see that." We follow the other shoppers up one of the three sets of escalators, eyeing the pretty billboards advertising expensive clothing and jewelry along the way. I step up a couple steps ahead of Jeremy and turn around to face him, giving him a good kiss on the lips. We cause some people around us to talk, but I don't care. This is a good man, and I'm proud of it. "I couldn't have asked for a better gift. Thank you, Jeremy."

"You're welcome." He returns the affection on the last set of moving stairs before we get off, officially entering the outside shopping mecca for the well-to-do. Whether by the beach or in the middle of the city, white folks know how to spend some money, and I'm not mad at them.

"Pretzels!" I exclaim, speed walking toward the cart. This should hold me over until dinner. Jeremy follows behind me, laughing at my excitement.

"There's a Tiffany's to your right and a Coach store to your left, and this is your first choice?" Jeremy continues to laugh at my hunger, but he knows how I am about food.

"Whatever. I told you I was hungry," I say, instinctively pulling out my coin purse from inside the Lucky bag, also a gift from my baby when we first started dating. He's always spoiled me, even if it has taken some getting used to.

"Your money's no good today, birthday girl," Jeremy says,

pulling his wallet from the back pocket of his worn Levi's and ordering two of the warm, twisted treats.

"You're too good to me," I say, taking the salty snack and strolling down the brightly lit corridors, ready to spend some more of his money. A girl could really get used to this type of treatment.

Yes, she can, my mom says, all up in our moment. *This is just the beginning. Once you get a taste of really being treated like a queen, you can never go back, nor should you. Have fun, baby. Like I said last night, you deserve a day to celebrate you, and I'm glad Jeremy thinks so, too.*

Thanks, Mom, I think back, trying not to look too obvious. Jeremy's just getting used to the idea of my family's religion. I have to ease him into the details of my lineage and our powers. We continue to walk and eat, taking in all the pretty things to pick from.

"Oooo, look at this," I say, eyeing the new line of Victoria's Secret bras in the store window. It's been a long time since I had a nice bra. I've had to settle for the department-store brands, and I'm sick of my breasts looking like pyramids underneath my shirts.

"Yeah, I'd love to see that on you," Jeremy says, eyeing a gown that leaves very little to the imagination.

"Down, boy," I say, leading him into the fancy underwear shop. We've got less than three hours before the stores close, and I'm ready to do some serious damage. I want to get my gifts' worth out of this trip. But before I can get too into the spree, my phone vibrates inside my purse. With my free hand, I take out the cell and flip it open to see yet another text from Nellie about the baby shower, insisting that we wear the matching outfits she picked out. I'll be so glad when this damn thing is over tomorrow, I don't know what to do. Everyone and their mama will be there—literally. Once I agreed to go along with Mrs. Esop's debutante plan, she graciously allowed us to use her backyard for the shower, if it doesn't rain. We'll see how it goes. I have two clients in the morning and will go shopping for the food afterward. I'm committed to doing my part for the festivities, but tonight it's all about me, and no one's getting my attention but Jeremy. Everything else can wait until tomorrow.

~ 8 ~
Backyard Boogie

"Gangstas don't dance, we boogie."

—MACK 10

After my clients left this morning, I cleaned up the house and observed my shopping treasures from last night's adventure. Jeremy and I had so much fun, we didn't get in until two in the morning. We spent so much money, I had to eventually stop reading the tags. I even bought the same outfit Nellie wants us to wear to the shower this afternoon, but in blue instead of yellow. I'm giving in, but not without maintaining some of my individuality. It's bad enough I have to spend my birthday weekend at my girl's ghetto-ass baby shower, but I also have to spring for half the food because I'm one of the godmothers. What the hell is wrong with this picture? And I know Rah's salty ass will be there because he's the godfather, no doubt. This should be the liveliest baby shower ever.

Jeremy left early this morning because he needed to shower and change before coming with me to Nigel's. We slept together last night without even coming close to having sex, and it was nice. Jeremy and I are learning to trust each other more every day, and because of that, I think I'm ready to tell him I love him, too. He hasn't said it again verbally, but he shows his love in little and big ways every day.

By the time Jeremy arrives, I'm ready to go. Nellie's handling the chicken and side dishes, and I'm responsible for the fish and salad. Nigel's providing the drinks, and Mickey's parents paid for the cake, even though they won't be able to make an appearance because they both have to work. With five children and a grandchild on the way, her parents can't afford to take any days off.

"So what's on the list?" Jeremy asks as we walk downstairs toward his car parked in the driveway. When my daddy does that shit, it pisses me off because I think it's rude to block the only way in or out of the carport. But it doesn't bother me as much when Jeremy does it, maybe because I know he's attempting chivalry and not because he's rushing me.

"I need to get fish and salad for the party and a few things for myself. The only problem is that I don't know where to get fresh seafood and the things I need all in the same place." I usually go to the Ralphs in the Ladera Center to get my groceries, but I've never been fond of buying fish from a large chain. Mama's got people all around the neighborhood who provide her with salmon straight off the line; I have no idea where there's a fish market around here.

"There's a farmer's market by my house that has great fresh fish and probably everything else you'll need." Jeremy backs out of the tight space, expertly avoiding the concrete walls on either side of us.

"All the way out there?" I ask, looking at the clock on the dashboard. It's already after twelve, and the party is supposed to start at two. If I'm late, Nellie will have a conniption, and I don't want to hear her mouth any more than it's already going to be running. The way she's invested her time, energy, and Nigel's money into this party, you'd think it was her own baby about to be born.

"Trust me, it'll be worth it," Jeremy says, reassuring me that the hour alone we'll spend driving back and forth makes sense. "I'll have you there on time, I promise. Don't you trust me?"

"More than you know," I say, letting Jeremy take the lead. I wanted to talk to him about what didn't happen between us last night anyway, and this drive will give us plenty of time to chat. "How come you didn't try to sleep with me last night? Not that I wanted you to or anything, but I'm just curious," I say, shifting uncomfortably in the leather seat. That sounded better when I said it in my head.

"I thought we did sleep with each other last night, or was that my other girlfriend snoring loudly on the floor beside me?" Jeremy's got jokes this afternoon, but I'm serious, no matter how awkward the conversation may be. We need to talk about sex and, considering we're on our way to a sixteen-year-old's baby shower, this is the perfect time to have the discussion. No matter how nice the party, I'd much rather be looking forward to my birthday next week than a baby shower any day.

"Come on, Jeremy," I say, tickling the side of his leg through his jeans. "You know what I mean. You're not a virgin, and I know you're feeling me, so what gives?"

"First of all, you *are* a virgin, and I don't want to rush you," he says, looking both ways before proceeding through the four-way stop. I like that he's always careful. "Besides, abstinence is the best policy against unwanted pregnancy, and I don't want to make that mistake again." I knew his runaway baby-mama had something to do with his decision not to push the sexual envelope with me. I never thought of his relationship with Tania as a positive for us until now. It's nice to know we're both on the same page about this.

"I agree one hundred percent," I say, holding Jeremy's right hand in my left as we enjoy the mellow ride to Redondo Beach. Enough said. Jeremy and I have a good time together, no matter what we're doing. Who needs the drama sex brings anyway? I'm good right where we are, and I'm glad Jeremy feels the same way.

"Welcome to Mrs. Wright's Farmer's Market," Jeremy says, turning off Pacific Coast Highway and into a large shopping plaza with several other small specialty stores neighboring our destination. The hippie-looking grocery store is very popular; customers are packed in the wide parking lot on foot and in their vehicles. Some folks are even riding bikes through the crowded space. Jeremy finds a spot at the back near the transplanted palm trees surrounding the property and decides to swoop it up before somebody else gets it. We may be far away from the entrance, but we're on a tight schedule and don't have the time to scout for a closer space.

As we step into the massive store, the first thing I notice to my left is the meat department, with one of the cleanest-looking seafood selections I've ever seen. I wish we could get good fish like this in my hood.

"Maybe I should do the rest of my shopping real quick before buying the fish," I say, eyeing all the pretty choices through the glass. There are so many to choose from—salmon, whiting, cod, and other varieties I've never heard of. The prices are even less expensive pound for pound than we pay in Compton. I think I'm in love at first sight with Mrs. Wright's.

"They can put it on ice for you so you don't have to get back in line, if you want," Jeremy says, glancing at the six people in front of us. "As a matter of fact, just give me your list, and I'll get everything else while you stay here. That should save us some time, too." Jeremy's such a good boyfriend. What did I ever do to deserve him?

"That's so sweet," I say, handing him the paper. "Are you sure you don't mind getting number six?" I ask as he deciphers my nearly illegible handwriting. Mama gets on me about my penmanship all the time. She says future generations won't be able to read my additions in the spirit book if I don't improve my script.

"It's cool; I've got a mom," Jeremy says, not even giving a second thought to being seen with my maxi pads. He is a keeper. If this is what a real partnership is, I like it. Having Jeremy around makes everything easier, almost too easy. Sometimes I feel a little guilty about all the privileges I have as his girlfriend and wonder if I'm taking advantage of the situation. No one has ever taken me on a shopping spree or to the restaurants that Jeremy can afford. Last night we ate at the Chart House in Malibu, a restaurant where nothing on the menu was below fifty dollars. It took everything in me not to put the rolls in one of the soft cloth napkins and slide them into my purse. I'm not used to this shit, but I'm going to have to work on it. This is Jeremy's world, and living in it with him comes with all the perks thereof.

Jeremy and I made it in and out of the store in twenty minutes with everything I needed accounted for. I have to say I like the carefree lifestyle these beach residents seem to have going on. It didn't even bother me that Mrs. Wright's carries only its own brand of my monthly necessities. I'm willing to try anything once, as long as they get the basic job done.

"I need to separate my personal things from the party stuff real quick. I might forget to do it once we get to Nigel's," I say, sorting through the items in the trunk. I spent damn near all my money on my groceries and Mickey's stuff. I saved just enough to get gas and my school snacks for the week. Not working my regular hours at Netta's is really hurting my bank account, but that'll change once I'm through this stressful school period.

"We have to leave now if we want to make it on time, babe," Jeremy says, returning the basket to the designated area. As one of the hostesses, I technically should've been there by now, as I'm sure Nellie will remind me of, once we finally do arrive.

"Damnit. They forgot to put the fish in the basket," I say, searching frantically through the multiple bags. "I'll have to go back in and get it." I take the receipt out of my purse on my arm and close the trunk. Now we're really going to be late.

"I'll be right here unless you want me to come with you." Holding hands, we walk around to the front of the car, where Jeremy gives me a quick kiss, bringing me back to center.

"I think I can handle it, but thanks anyway, Big Daddy." Jeremy laughs at my sass, watching me walk back across the crowded parking lot and into the packed store with my receipt in hand. This shouldn't take too long, and the fish was on ice. It should have been pretty obvious to the cashier that it was left behind.

"Excuse me, miss," I say, spotting the store manager at the customer-service desk and politely catching her attention. Luckily, this is the only register without a long line. "Less than ten minutes ago I was at register four, and the fish I purchased wasn't in the basket when I got to the car," I say, pointing to the register behind me. I notice that it's closed, and the cashier is nowhere in sight. What the hell?

"Okay, I'll check the register to see if anything was left. Our policy is that if a customer leaves any items behind after paying for them, they are left up here, and I haven't received anything in the last ten minutes." The petite blond woman walks around the enclosed area and through the small swinging door that separates her cubicle from the main floor. She heads over to the vacant register and sees the same thing I see: nothing.

"What happened to my fish?" I ask the manager, but she looks unconcerned. "Here's my receipt. Thirty dollars' worth of whiting didn't just disappear," I add, reading her expression. I know this trick thinks I'm lying, but I've got the proof right here.

"Like I said, if anything was left behind, it would be in here with me." She steps back into her safe space, dismissing my receipt and claim with the lock of the door. This trick's about to bring out the gangster in me. I don't care what zip code we're presently in.

"You can see I just made my purchase. I'm not leaving until I get my food or my money back." The people around us notice the tension in my voice and look at the angry black girl in the store. Shit, they'd be angry, too, if it was their money and time wasted. But then again, if I were one of the white or Asian customers, we wouldn't be having this conversation.

"I'm sorry, but I can't do that." The manager's thin nose crinkles in a look of disgust at my receipt and behavior, but she hasn't seen anything yet.

"What do you mean you can't do that?" I ask, completely insulted. If this were a Pavilions or Ralphs, there would be no problem, but the customer service at this market is a little different.

"We can't refund you based on he say/she say. Maybe you left it in the cart." This woman has got to be out of her mind to think I wouldn't notice leaving a cold, heavy-ass bag in the grocery basket.

"Or maybe she took my fish home to feed her family." I need that food for the party, and I don't have another thirty dollars. What am I going to do?

"Babe, what's taking so long?" Jeremy asks, walking into the store and making his way through the crowd to where I'm standing near tears, I'm so frustrated.

"The bag is gone, and so is all my money," I say, burying my head in his chest. He strokes my fresh cornrows that I just braided this morning and hugs me tightly.

"Okay, Jayd, just calm down," Jeremy says. "Hey, Mrs. Henry." He greets the store manager like she's one of his teachers.

"You two know each other?" she asks, shocked. I raise my head from Jeremy's polo shirt to watch the two of them interact, observing her stance relax—unlike the defensive posture she immediately took with me. Oh, I see, it's like that. Sometimes I want to whip a heffa's ass just because she—or he—is expecting it.

"Yeah," Jeremy says. The bitch is all smiles, now that Jeremy's a part of the conversation. "This is my girlfriend, Jayd. She goes to South Bay, too."

"I didn't know she was a friend of yours, Jeremy," Mrs. Henry says, taking the receipt from my hand and writing on it. "I'm sorry for the confusion. Take that to the seafood department, and they'll issue you another portion." Unbelievable. All the crying in the world wouldn't have saved the day, but my rich white boyfriend walks in, and it's all good.

"Thanks, Mrs. Henry," Jeremy says, completely unaware of what just happened. "I'll get it, Jayd. I pulled up in front of the store." He gestures toward the double doors. "Why don't you go chill in the car before they tow it, and then we'll really be in trouble." I doubt he'd get towed, because I have a feeling Jeremy's good luck works with law enforcement, too. How truly privileged Jeremy's world really is.

The thirty-minute ride back to Los Angeles is quiet, mostly because I have nothing to say. I'm so upset about what just went down at the market, but I don't know how to explain it to Jeremy. I'd rather deal with the expensive prices and fewer choices at the markets in Compton than deal with the racist bull in Jeremy's neck of the woods any day. Jeremy probably thinks I'm being overemotional as usual, but I don't think so. If I have to face his reality, he's going to have to deal with mine, too.

When we arrive at Nigel's house, there are about two dozen

cars parked along the spacious block. It looks like the entire Westingle and South Bay crews have shown up for the festivities. The deejay's music can be heard from the gated entrance leading into Nigel's fancy hood. I know Nellie has games and other traditional baby-shower activities planned, but, ultimately, this is Mickey and Nigel's day, and I know the party's going to be off the chain.

"So are you going to tell me what's wrong before we get inside?" Jeremy asks, parking the car in the driveway behind Nigel's green Impala and Chance's Nova. Rah's ride is parked at the very front of the driveway. He's probably been here all day helping set up.

"It's complicated," I say, walking around to the trunk and taking out a few of the bags. Jeremy gets the rest and closes the trunk. I can smell the chicken on the grill, causing my stomach to growl. It won't take but a minute to prepare the fish, and after all I've been through to get it, it had better be the best damn whiting ever.

"Jayd, why are you so mad at me when I just got your food back? Isn't that what you wanted?" Jeremy asks, following me through the side gate and toward the kitchen door. Nellie gave me explicit instructions to enter through this way so we can make our grand entrance outside together. She's really taking this party-planning thing too far, but she wouldn't be Nellie if she didn't.

"Yes, you did, and I appreciate it," I say, stopping before opening the door. I look up at Jeremy and into his blue eyes, wondering if he will ever understand what I go through as a black girl in his city. "I'm not mad at you, Jeremy. I'm mad at this dumb-ass society."

"Well, that's just stupid, Jayd, and a waste of time. It's a big society, or haven't you learned anything from studying for the microeconomics AP?" Jeremy smiles, trying to make light of the situation.

"Stupid to you because you get all the benefits of your birthright without a second thought. I should've been able to get the fish back by my damn self, Jeremy. But my black word wasn't good enough for your homegirl, the manager." I shift the bags in my hands. They're becoming heavier with each passing minute we stand here, debating this issue. Noticing my discomfort, Jeremy reaches out to me with both hands and takes my bags, now carrying the full load. From the first day Jeremy and I started talking, he's always been a gentleman—carrying my books for me, opening doors, all that. Our only issue has to do with race, and it's a big one for me.

"I think you're overreacting, babe. It was just a misunderstanding," he says, trying to hug me, but I back away from his embrace.

"And, as usual, you're underreacting. It's not always my fault, Jeremy." He looks truly hurt by my words. I focus on the tiny silver flecks in his dark blue eyes, feeling the inside of his mind cool to my entrance. Jeremy's mind is unusually chilly to me, with no obvious reaction to my anger whatsoever. He truly does want me to be happy, and that, in his mind, starts with me not taking everything so personally. I agree with him, but he also needs to see the flip side, which I can thankfully show him better than I can tell him.

"I'm sorry, Jayd. I know sometimes people can treat you unfairly simply because you're African American," Jeremy says, putting the rethought view into his own words. My mom's powers are so dope. I hope I can keep them indefinitely. If Mama finds out about it, she'll definitely strip me of them, and I see why. In the wrong hands, the ability to change someone's point of view can be a very dangerous thing.

"Thank you, baby. That's all I wanted to hear," I say, reaching my neck up to meet Jeremy's lips. I slowly release my thoughts from his, kissing him without regard to where we are. There's another gate separating the backyard from where we're standing, and anyone could walk out the door or through either gate at any time.

"That was totally weird," Jeremy says, moving away from my lips and kissing me on the nose. "I feel like I just had a brain freeze, even though I didn't have anything cold to drink."

"Yeah, totally weird. Maybe it's all the ice you're carrying." I kiss my man again, enjoying the peace before the looming chaos awaiting us inside. I didn't mean to jump into his head, so I don't feel like I have anything to confess. Hopefully, one day I'll be able to tell Jeremy about all my tricks, but not today. Interrupting our quiet time, Rah opens the kitchen door holding a large aluminum pan full of meat. Rah looks as uncomfortable as I feel. I wish I could jump into his mind right now, but no such luck.

"What's up, man," Jeremy says, the first to break the ice. I haven't even told him about the argument Rah and I are currently engaged in, nor does it matter. Jeremy already knows we've got ongoing issues.

"What's up?" Rah says, passing us and heading toward the back, where the grill is. Nigel's mom and dad had the back-yard redone and installed a permanent grill on the outdoor-patio portion of the large space. There's also a basketball court, Jacuzzi, and grass area for lying out. From the sound of it, the party's in full swing. Jeremy and I walk into the buzzing kitchen and spot Nigel's mom entering the large room on the other side like a banker checking on her invest-ment. I would be, too, with all these unfamiliar people around here.

"Jayd, it's about time you got here," Nellie says from her stance at the kitchen table, her loyal boyfriend sitting right beside her.

"What's up, Jeremy? Jayd, do you know you two are dressed alike?" Chance asks, being funny. He's well aware of Nellie's control issues. I glance around, looking for Mickey and Nigel, who aren't in here, but there are several people I do recognize from school; they say hi. They must be some of Nellie's freshmen ASB worker-bee recruits. I have to admit—everything looks well organized, just like Nellie planned. She must be ecstatic it all worked out so well.

"Hi, everyone," I say, waving to Mrs. Esop, who smiles my way. Jeremy puts his bags on the floor next to the long island in the middle of the kitchen and walks over to greet Chance. Rah walks back into the kitchen, stepping up right behind me. The last thing I need is his shit right now.

"So, y'all are pretty tight now, huh?" Rah says, whispering over my head. "You give it up yet?" I look back at him, ready to slap the black off his chiseled onyx face. Rah has let his jealousy get the best of him, and it's very unattractive.

"Jayd, we're going outside to say what's up to the mom-and dad-to-be," Jeremy says.

"Okay. I'll be out when I finish up in here," I say, moving away from Rah and placing the bags on the island, ready to prepare my portion of the feast.

"Okay, but don't take too long. I need your help with the gifts before we make our entrance," Nellie says, eyeing her checklist. She hasn't even commented on my outfit, she's so busy. Chance gets up from the table to escort Jeremy out. Nellie and her helpers follow them into the living room but take a right instead of heading outside with our boys. I wish Rah would join them, but he's too busy bothering me. Thank goodness Mrs. Esop is still in the room. I know he won't get too crazy with his second mom around.

"Jayd, it's always so lovely to see you, dear," Mrs. Esop says, stepping between Rah and me before I can cuss him out. I return her affection and stick my tongue out at Rah, who's standing behind us. "And, Rah, where's that beautiful baby of yours?" She turns around and hugs Rah, too. I roll my eyes and continue unpacking my groceries, realizing that a few of my personal groceries will need to be kept cold if I expect to use them in the future.

"She's fine," Rah says. "Sandy should be dropping her off soon." There's that name again, the main reason why Rah should be mad and not hating on my happiness.

"Mrs. Esop, do you mind if I store a few things in your refrigerator until after the party?" I ask. She has turned her focus outside. There must be at least fifty people in her backyard, and the party just started.

"Sure, Jayd. I think there's some room at the bottom," Mrs. Esop says, pointing to the refrigerator while staring out the kitchen window over the sink. I open one of the two stainless-steel drawers and place my items inside while eyeing their inventory. I bet they never go hungry in this house. "And is that your boyfriend, Jayd?"

Rah looks at me and smiles like I just got busted for doing something wrong. He can be so immature sometimes.

"Yes, his name is Jeremy." I close the drawers and proceed to the sink to wash my hands and get started on the food. The grill smells good, but I can't help worrying about the weather. I guess if it does start to rain we can move the party inside, but I doubt Mrs. Esop will go for that. Her house is not the place to house teenagers and barbecue sauce at the same time.

"Interesting," she says, moving away from the window and toward the main entrance adjacent to the living room. "Well, I'll leave you all to your baby shower, if this counts as my appearance, Jayd." Mrs. Esop thinks she's slick. The deal we made stated that she would make an appearance at Mickey's shower if I agreed to let her sponsor me as a debutante for her sorority. And appear at the shower, she did. That's probably why she agreed to let us have it here. Before I can respond, she's through the living room and up the stairs on her way to her third-story getaway. The master bedroom takes up the entire floor, leaving Nigel's room, his sister's room, and the other three unfinished rooms on the second floor alone. It must be nice to have more space than you know what to do with.

"You didn't answer my question, so it must be true." Rah wastes no time getting back on my case about Jeremy. I take one of the three aluminum trays on the counter and spread out the fish to season. I'll prepare the salad last. Rah's unrelenting in his stare. If I didn't know better, I'd say he was the one with the powerful sight.

"Rah, if you must know, we're abstinent. Jeremy believes the only surefire way against pregnancy is not to have sex, and I happen to agree," I say, sprinkling garlic powder and other good stuff over the food. I'm not ready to get on the pill or even entertain other birth-control options right now.

"That's the dumbest shit I've ever heard," Rah says, taking the bags of ice in the smaller sink next to the stove and placing them in one of the large coolers on the floor. There's enough soda in there to last for days, and that's only one of the three I see in the kitchen. I knew Rah would see Jeremy and me abstaining from sex as a way to challenge the authenticity of our bond.

"Not that I care what you think, but what Jeremy and I have is real—trust—and I don't need to prove it to anyone, least of all to you, who should be on a warning billboard for the perils of teenage sex."

Undeterred by my words, Rah keeps his eyes locked on me. "I know you care. You can't lie to me, Jayd, or have you forgotten?" Rah walks toward me, getting right up in my face.

If my hands weren't dirty, I'd push him away from me, but I can't. "If you want to stay friends with me, you will respect my man. I've been too nice about it, but if we have to get dirty about it, so be it." I put my hands out in front of me, ready to mess up his clean shirt, and he backs away. Interrupting us, Nellie storms into the kitchen with Mickey waddling right behind her. Let the games begin.

"Hey, Mickey. Nellie, I'm almost done in here," I say, returning my focus to my duties and away from Rah and his tempting cologne. Why does he always get under my skin? Deciding he's had enough drama before it even begins, Rah exits through the back door with the cooler in tow.

"Forget about the damn food," Mickey says, taking everyone aback. If Mickey's dismissing food, I know this must be serious.

"Some niggas from the hood are here," Mickey says, all stressed out. "I know Nellie didn't tell them where Nigel lived, so it had to be you!" Mickey screams at me, forgetting that Nigel's parents are home. All they need is another reason to call Mickey unsuitable for their son, and a fight at their house with her in it will do.

"You need to slow your roll, girl. I don't know how those fools knew about the party, but I sure as hell didn't tell them," I say, washing my hands in the sink. I take a few paper towels off the roll on the counter and cover the tray, ready to take it outside. I can see through the window that there are several people from Westingle I want to avoid at all costs. I'm surprised Nigel's ex-girlfriend Tasha isn't here with her best friend, and Rah's ex-girlfriend, Trish, but it's still early in the afternoon. The black crew from South Bay has come out, Misty and KJ included. I can also see that most of the football and basketball teams from both schools have shown up. Our boys are chilling outside while the heat is definitely on in this kitchen.

"Jayd, please," Mickey says, her hands on her hips, extensions swinging. "Who else would know them and Nigel?" Nellie looks like she's about to pass out, she's so upset. I guess this wasn't the type of guest list she had in mind. Did we forget who the guest of honor is? Mickey—a notorious thug's estranged girlfriend. Folks from around our way were surely going to want to drop by if they could get a ride, some of whom obviously did.

"Mickey, seriously. Why in the hell would I want them fools to know where Nigel lives? He's my friend, too, you know," I say, taking a wooden serving bowl out of the cabinet above the stove for the salad. "As a matter of fact, he was my friend first." Mickey's eyes narrow at the truth. Good. Maybe that'll shut her up before I throw this bowl at her head.

"I invited them," Mickey's little brother Mikey says, walking into the kitchen with half of Mickey's man's gang behind him. "I thought they had a right to come because they're good friends with the baby-daddy." Mikey has gone too far this time.

"Mikey, you know Nigel ain't friends with none of these fools," Mickey says, but we both know he's not referring to Nigel. The paternity of Mickey's baby has always been questionable.

"And who invited you?" Nellie asks. "You're not on my list." This is the angriest I've ever seen my girl, whose dark brown skin looks radiant in her yellow shirt. I guess she figured one thing should match her new hairdo.

"I don't need no invitation. I'm the uncle. I've got rights, too, you know." Mikey looks around Nigel's kitchen in awe of the lavish detail and state-of-the-art appliances. "How much you think I can get for that blender?"

"Nothing—now go home," Mickey says, snatching her brother's hand away from the expensive equipment and pushing him toward the door. His homies laugh as she tries to move their boy. An eighth grader, Mikey could easily pass for a sophomore in high school. Mikey started banging with Mickey's man a couple years ago when Mickey and her man were hanging real tight. She has no one to blame for where

Mikey's loyalties now lie but herself—and maybe her parents for letting her date a gangster in the first place.

"Go home? But the party's just getting started, big sis." Mikey takes a forty-ounce of Olde English beer from the brown paper bag he's holding and begins drinking it. Mickey better hope Mrs. Esop doesn't walk in on this shit. She'll call the police in a heartbeat, no matter whose brother he is.

"Oh, my God," Nellie says, waving her hands in the air in complete melodramatic fashion. I agree this is a mess, but acting like Erica Kane isn't going to get us anywhere.

"Look, y'all, this is a private gathering on private property," I say in an attempt to bring some much needed perspective into the room. "I suggest y'all get out of here before Nigel's parents find out you've brought alcohol to a teenage party. They'll have no problem pressing charges against all y'all." I know they don't care about getting caught by adults, but they do care about getting busted over something like this. Each of these four fools has a rap sheet as long as Nellie's weave.

"Hey, Jayd. You look good in them jeans, girl," Mikey says, already faded. "When you gon' let a nigga hit?" While thinking of an equally offensive comeback to this little boy's question, I feel my mom's cool eyes begin to take over my own. I look into Mikey's thoughts and change what he sees. *You will leave this house now*, I say, before unexpectedly letting go. Mikey looks back at his crew, dressed from top to bottom in black except for the red rag they each have hanging from their back pockets, and then back at me, confused about what I know he's thinking.

"Are you wearing blue, fool?" one of Mikey's friends says to me. Mikey looks more mellow, but his boy's question seems to take him right back to where we started, and his crew is there with him.

"I'm not a fool, fool, and I can wear whatever I want." Nellie and Mickey both look at me like I'm the baddest bitch ever, and I admit, that's exactly how I feel. My mom's powers are having a serious effect on my self-esteem.

"You got a big mouth on you for someone so little," he says, taking a step toward me; but Mikey stops him in his tracks.

"Nah, man. She's cool. If it weren't for her, Tre would never have gotten the props he deserved at his funeral." Mikey's friend looks like he wants to smack the shit out of me, and I wish he would. I've got several different ways I can work these salad tongs to my advantage if I need to. His friend looks down at my blue off-the-shoulder shirt and jeans with matching detail like a bull seeing red. I've never understood how someone could have so much loyalty to a color.

"Try me," I say, picking up the wooden spoon with fork attachment, ready to work them upside his head. Mickey looks mad as hell, but not at her brother's friend. Instead she's staring at me like I sold her out. What the hell?

"Let's go, dog. There ain't shit for us to do here, no way," Mikey says, leading the way out. I guess my thoughts did sink in after all. Nellie and I follow them out to make sure the boys leave.

"But what about honoring Tre's memory, dog? That's why we're here, ain't it?" Mikey's boy says. Tre's memory? What does Tre have to do with any of this? I know Mickey fooled around with him once or twice, but that was a long time ago, or was it?

"Get out of here now, Mikey. Damn, you have a big mouth!" Mickey shouts. I guess big mouths run in their family. Mickey pushes her brother out of the kitchen and toward the front door, but not without first taking a sip of his beer.

"All right, Mickey, damn. Can a nigga finish his drink first?"

"Drink? What kind of drink?" Mrs. Esop says, coming down the stairs and meeting the uninvited guest in the foyer.

"Oh, it's just a little Olde E," Mikey says, not realizing he just ended the party for his sister in more ways than one. Mrs. Esop looks at Mickey with pure rage in her eyes and then back at her brother, whose friends are already out the door.

"You indignant little hoodlum. Nigel, get these people out of my house!" Mrs. Esop yells, practically running out the patio door. Mikey exits the front door, leaving me, Nellie, and Mickey alone in the room.

"This was all a part of your master plan to break up Nigel and me once and for all, I know it," Mickey says to me, now completely irrational. Nellie silently watches us go at it, upset that she's no longer in control of today's festivities.

"Why would I do that?" I ask, heading back into the kitchen, but I've just about had it with defending myself against my own girls. "Trust me, Mickey. I want you and Nigel to be together just as much as you do."

"Oh, please, Jayd. You don't give a damn about anyone but yourself," Mickey says, rolling her neck. "What, you think you're white now because you got a white boyfriend and new friends, staying up all night drinking coffee and talking about books and shit? Get a grip, fool. You still live in the hood, and I know you know better than to wear the wrong colors."

"Whatever, Mickey," I say, ready to clock her ass. But I have to think about the baby, not her. "How was I supposed to know your brother and his gang were going to show up?" Nellie looks at me as if to say *I told you to wear yellow* but doesn't say a word. Since when did being original become a crime?

"Jayd, I know you can't wait to tell Nigel I slept with Tre. It'll support his mama's theory that I'm nothing but a slut and you're the Virgin freaking Mary," she says, not realizing

Nigel, Rah, Chance, Jeremy, and Nigel's mom have reentered the room behind her.

"You did what?" Nigel asks, dropping the liter of Coke he's carrying on the cream-colored carpet. Thank God for plastic bottles. Nigel looks around at us all, completely embarrassed and hurt. He runs past us and out the front door, with Rah right behind him. Jeremy and I look at each other in recognition that our no-sex plan is definitely the best policy for us. Chance and Nellie are already sleeping together, but, hopefully, they're having second thoughts about their love life, too.

"This is all your fault," Mickey says with tears of fear and pain in her eyes. I can feel her daughter's panic from inside the womb, but there's nothing I can do to help my godchild. I'm not doing a very good job at protecting Nickey Shantae, but, hopefully, I can fix this mess before she gets here. "Nigel, wait!" Mickey calls after him, but if I were her, I'd let him cool off a bit before trying to tell her side of this soap opera. Before she runs down the stairs after Nigel, she turns around and takes a final stab at me. "Did you tell Rah about how you left Rahima upstairs asleep with the door wide open?" Now that was cold, even for Mickey. Misty smiles through the glass door, marveling at what I assume is somehow her work. I'll deal with her later. The deejay is still spinning, but we've become the main attraction, and not how Nellie planned it.

"Jayd, what's she talking about?" Rah asks from the bottom of the porch steps where he and Nigel are standing. Nigel looks up at Mickey and shakes his head. Before I can answer either one of them, Nigel walks off, with Rah and Mickey following behind.

"I trust you all will clean up this mess and tell the rest of your friends the party's over," Mrs. Esop says, heading back upstairs. "And I look forward to seeing you at the debutante meet-and-greet in a couple weeks, Jayd." She got everything she wanted without having to lift a finger or break her word.

She's the coldest bitch I've ever met. We should take notes from her playbook. Mrs. Esop's swagger is so tight I know she's got haters wherever she goes. We'd better get to work putting her house back in order, as there's no fixing the mess Mickey's made. I feel sorry for my girl, but no matter what she thinks, this isn't my fault. She made her bed, and now she's got to sleep in it, no matter how uncomfortable it may be.

~ 9 ~
Seventeen Candles

"Am I a part of the cure /
Or am I part of the disease."

—COLDPLAY

Since Sunday's horrific barbecue, Mickey has been in rare hater form for the past two days. Luckily, I've been so preoccupied with my own shit it's been easy to avoid the madness. Nigel's mad at Mickey, Mickey's mad at me, and I don't know what to do. Lucky for me, Jeremy's kept me on my game academically by making sure I don't miss a single study session. The APs have provided the perfect distraction from everything else until I can find a solution to the madness.

Thank God for the regular faculty short Tuesdays, which provided an early escape from today's school bull. And Misty's still due a good cussing out, but she's been absent all week. Misty's done some evil shit in her day, but telling everyone in class about me leaving Rah's daughter alone during an incident that she indirectly caused is the epitome of low. And Mickey repeating the shit in front of Rah on Sunday was icing on the cake for the heffa. What I want to know is exactly how Misty's doing her dirty work this time. Maybe Mama can give me some insight when I get to the shop this afternoon. She's still upset with me for moving out, but Mama can never turn away from me when I need her help.

It's been interesting running errands for Mama, now that

I can drive, and she's taken full advantage of it since I've moved out, too. Because of the spiritual initiation she's participating in next month, Mama's had to outsource a lot of her usual work to get ready for the festivities. The priest she's sending me to this afternoon lives all the way on the other side of town in Long Beach. At least Mama said she would reimburse me for gas money when I get to the shop this afternoon. This morning was the first time she ever called and asked about the early Tuesday school schedule. I should've known then she wanted me to do something for her with my extra afternoon hours.

When I arrive at the old house, it immediately gives me the creeps. I ring the front doorbell and see an older Latina woman in the living room. The elder doesn't move from her spot on the ancient sofa and points me to the back of the house. She must know why I'm here. I walk around the unkempt front porch and notice a raggedy chain-link fence separating the main house from a small backhouse, much like the one where Mama houses her spirit room. But unlike our yard, this grass hasn't seen the blade of a lawn mower in quite some time. There's trash strewn everywhere, and there's no clear path to get to the front door of the little house.

"Shit," I say, realizing I've stepped in a big pile of dog mess hidden in the tall grass. How did I miss that?

"There's a tree branch and a water hose to your right. Clean your feet before stepping foot on my porch," a man's voice says from behind the dirty screen door. I can't make out his face, but I see where he's pointing, and I follow his directions. I'm glad I wore my sneakers today because if I were in my sandals, we'd be having a totally different conversation.

I get my shoes as clean as I can and continue with my mission. I don't know what I'm picking up, but I hope it's ready to go because I am. And a sistah is hungry. There was so much food left over from the baby shower I could eat for a week off the leftovers alone.

Without coming all the way outside, the tall, slender black man with multiple scars on his face opens the screen door, hands me a large paper bag, and relocks the door. From the looks of the yard, I didn't want to come in anyway.

"Thank you," I say, turning around to leave. Whatever's in this bag is heavy, and it's going to be a challenge maneuvering through the poopie-trapped grass and not dropping what I came here for.

"Be careful with that, girl!" the old man yells at me, causing me to jump. Damn, he didn't have to say it like that. "And tell Queen Jayd this makes us even, yeah?" It always throws me off when people call Mama by her voodoo title from New Orleans, but from this elder's thick accent that I can't place, I'd say he knows Mama from way back when.

"Okay," I say, almost to my car parked in the driveway. I can still feel his eyes on me as I open the door and place the bag on the passenger's seat. I'm glad that's over. Luckily, I have some notebook paper to put my messed-up Nikes on. I have an extra pair of sandals at Netta's. I can't wait to get to the shop and make some money. Too bad no customers are going to be there this afternoon because it's Mama's day in the chair. But at least I'll be able to get out of work that much faster and to my study group. I already called my mom for her birthday today, and she was thrilled, mostly because her man has big plans for her tonight. I hope she enjoys it because once Mama finds out that she's ditching us for her man, her mood will surely change.

It took me longer than usual to get here because rather than take the side streets, I decided to jump on the 710 freeway, thinking it would be faster, which was a huge mistake.

There were so many trucks on the raggedy-ass highway I couldn't move very fast. When I finally did arrive at the shop, Mama met me outside to retrieve the goods and take them straight to the back. Whatever's in that bag must be important. I'm touched that Mama still trusts me to handle serious stuff, even if she barely looked at me when I spoke. But Netta's as warm as ever, and I'm grateful for the positive energy. We've had a lively afternoon so far, and Netta looks especially radiant after Mama hooked her hair up last week. If Mama was in the business of doing hair again, we wouldn't be able to keep up with the clientele.

Because the conversation has been civilized, I think it's a good time to request that Mama and Netta show up for my speech on Sunday, even though I know it's a long shot. I also asked my mom to come, and after much begging on my part, she finally agreed. I know it'll be a sacrifice to humble themselves and make an appearance among their enemies, but I need their moral support.

"Will you be able to come to Daddy's church on Easter Sunday for my speech?" They both stop what they're doing and look up at me briefly, rolling their eyes. Mama sucks her teeth in disgust. Netta cleans her station, and I fold the clean laundry, waiting for their next move. I wish I could jump into Mama's mind, but I already know my mom's tricks don't work on her.

"Be careful what you say up on that pulpit, Jayd," Mama says, pushing the hair drier off her head. "You know our great ancestor Tituba was burned at the stake for our ways, and no matter what the history books say, it wasn't that long ago." Mama's always got to be so cryptic with her shit. It's just a little speech at the church, not a seminar on how to be a voodoo priestess.

"Yes, girl. They do love them some Jesus up in that little church house. Try not to say anything that will offend them,"

Netta says, spraying more of her all-natural cleansing and disinfectant solution onto the booth and wiping it down before Mama takes her place in the chair. I know she's being serious because I've seen the way Daddy looks at Mama whenever she brings up him not honoring his ancestors. She blames his lack of respect for what we do for my uncles' issues, and Daddy says if she'd stayed in the church, everything would be the way it was when they first got married, which to him was all good.

"Oh, there's nothing really wrong with them loving their Jesus," Mama says. "It's just the other folks they forget to equally love in the process that concerns me." Me too. I'm doing this only because Daddy asked me to, and I want to make him proud. In his eyes, I'll always be his "Tweet," and because he's the only one who calls me by the nickname, I'd be hurt if I disappointed him like I did when I got into it with my uncle Kurtis last week. I thought for sure he'd change his mind about me speaking this Sunday, but no such luck.

"Exactly. Don't you get up there and start talking about the orisha, because it'll be over their heads. They might even consider it blasphemous and build a stake right there to burn you on." Netta can be so silly sometimes. She directs Mama to sit down in front of her so Netta can continue working her magic.

"They wouldn't need a stake," Mama says, returning the heaviness to the mood. "They'll use their words to light a fire up under your ass." Okay, now Mama's scaring me. Is it really that bad? I haven't been to church regularly since I was a little girl and don't remember witnessing most of Mama's drama, but I've heard about it all my life.

"Mama, I can handle it," I say, continuing with my folding at the empty station next to where they're seated. Mama looks up at me as Netta parts her shoulder-length salt-and-pepper tresses, glaring at my remark.

"A little taste of passion, and the girl's already smelling

herself," Mama says, flipping through her Victoria's Secret cat-
alog, reminding me of the spree Jeremy took me on on Sat-
urday. I still haven't opened all my bags but will get to them
by my birthday tomorrow. Somewhere in those bags is my
birthday outfit, fancy bra included. Before I can respond,
Netta gets a quick punch in, too.

"Just wait until she gets past the heavy petting," Netta
says. "She's really going to lose her mind." Are they spying on
me at my mom's house or what?

"Ms. Netta!" I say, shocked by her crass remark about my
presex life. "I can't believe you just said that to me." I place
clean towels at each of the stations, starting with the driers. I
may only be seventeen come tomorrow, but I deserve my privacy. That's why I moved out in the first place.

"Well, she did, and she wasn't talking to you," Mama says,
rolling her eyes at me. Her green eyes look bloodshot. If I
didn't know any better, I'd say she's been smoking weed
with the boys, but I know her red eyes are from lack of sleep.
I'm sure she's been restless ever since I left, and to tell the
truth, I haven't slept much either the past couple days. It's
one thing to be alone in my mom's apartment for the weekend, but all week is another thing entirely.

"Yes, womanhood is definitely creeping up on our little miss,
isn't it, Lynn Mae?" They both look at me through the mirror's
reflection at Netta's station, and I can't help but see the collective glow in their eyes. I stop what I'm doing and stare back,
overcome by the light.

"My mother is taking over. I can see it in her eyes," Mama
says, probing my eyes with hers. Netta lends Mama her sight,
and Mama goes full throttle on a sistah like never before. My
body stands upright at the sheer thrust of Mama's mind into
mine. What is she looking for, and how come she didn't just
ask for it? I can't move I'm so caught up in their rapture. I
hope she can't see my mom's powers while she's in there.

"Yes, Lynn Mae. Maman Marie is definitely making her presence known," Netta says, brushing Mama's hair without looking down. Their connection is always tight when Netta's doing Mama's hair, but this is a bit much for me today. I've still got so much studying to do, and I've got to drive back to Inglewood tonight. Can they let go already?

"All your gifts are manifesting before your eyes, Jayd, but don't get too full of yourself, or you'll lose them just like your mother did," Mama says as the vision of me doing Shawntrese's hair comes into focus. Instead of her hair looking radiant like it has since I've helped in her healing process, it's breaking off in my hand. If I could say something I'd scream out in horror. But all I can do is watch and wait to be released from the psychic lesson I'm being served.

"Our girl won't stray too far from home, will you, Jayd?" Ms. Netta asks, still stroking perfect waves into Mama's do. "You'll always stay close to home, no matter where you live." Finally, they let go of their hold, and I shake my head in amazement. The dazed look leaves their eyes, and they continue with their hair session as if nothing just happened.

"I feel dizzy," I say as they look at me like they didn't just tap into my thoughts. They both smile coyly, resuming their regular programming. I think they just put something on me, but I'm not sure. I'll have to look it up next time I'm in the spirit room, which won't be tonight. That's another thing about not living with Mama—I miss having access to our shrines and the spirit book all the time. But I can't go back to Compton—not now. Maybe after the APs are over I'll think about it. Besides, a girl can live off of leftovers for only so long. Mama's cooking is all the reason I need to move back home, but I'd never tell her that and admit defeat. A girl's got her pride, and like OutKast says, I've got to stay ice cold and on my game at all times if I want to make it through.

"Happy earthday, Jayd," Mama says, handing me a small

gold box from Netta's booth as I come to. Mama always calls our birthdays "earthdays" because she says our spirits were always in existence; therefore, the day we are physically born is not our actual birthday, just the day we make our appearance into this world. Mama has her own logic about everything, and most of the time it makes perfect sense.

I open the shiny box and notice the five green jade bangles we wear for spiritual protection inside, and there's also an oriki on a gold piece of paper lying underneath them in Netta's handwriting. I wonder what this is for. I look up at both of their reflections and don't know what to say. I want to be happy, but I'm not. I'm actually more disappointed at the inherited gift than anything. These bracelets are always on loan, so why is she giving them to me for my birthday?

"They're yours to keep now, little Miss Jayd. You'll need them now more than ever," Mama says, answering my silent question. Now she's talking. In that case, this is one of the best gifts I've ever received. I slip the delicate jewelry onto my left arm. They feel cool against my skin, reminding me of the first time I wore them to defend myself against Misty's madness.

"And the oriki is for your protection, too, little Miss Thang. When you feel overwhelmed or powerless, chant that for Baba Shango, and he will remove all obstacles from your path." Netta smiles as she removes the hair drape from around Mama's shoulders and shakes the excess hair onto the floor for me to sweep up later. Hopefully, they'll give me tomorrow off because it's my official special day. It's bad enough I have AP meetings during break and lunch; I shouldn't have to come in to work, too.

"Here's your gas money and a little something extra, too," Mama says, pulling a fifty-dollar bill from her bra—the safest wallet in the world—and handing it to me. "Food's expensive nowadays, isn't it, little Jayd?" I can't hide anything from

Mama. I don't know why I try to keep anything from her when I know it's no use.

"And enjoy your day tomorrow," Netta says, making sure she didn't miss a single strand on Mama's head. "We can handle the shop. You have fun with your friends." I wish that were possible. Unfortunately, I'll probably spend the day trying to avoid them as much as possible in order to keep my good mood.

"Thank you both very much," I say, hugging Mama first and then Netta. They never did answer me about coming to see me speak this weekend, but I know they will. They've always got my back and, unlike my friends, they never leave me in the dark. It'll be a miracle if Mickey and Nellie even remember it's my birthday tomorrow, but we'll see. I'm going to enjoy my day no matter what bull comes my way via friends, enemies, and everyone else in between.

After I left work yesterday evening, I stayed at the study session until midnight. At least it was at one of my favorite spots, the Coffee Bean & Tea Leaf. With all the caffeine in my system, I couldn't have slept even if I had made it back to Inglewood earlier. Jeremy has been the perfect gentleman, escorting me home every evening since I moved into my mom's place. He usually spends the night and leaves early in the morning to get ready for school at his own house. I'm glad for the company because I do get scared sleeping alone at night sometimes.

When I woke up this morning Jeremy had a bagel with a candle in the middle waiting for me on the dining room table. It was the sweetest thing ever, and the bagel was good, too. Today might just turn out to be the best birthday I've ever had. With Jeremy's thoughtfulness, it's already been perfect. My mom was the first one to greet me before I even woke up fully, singing "Happy Birthday" into my mind. I'm glad she and Karl are happy, but I do miss my mom being around, especially today.

My cell vibrates in my purse, beginning what I hope to be a day full of well wishes. I look at the caller ID and see it's my father calling. At least he didn't forget like he usually does. He can never remember whose birthday comes first—my mother's or mine—and usually ends up calling me on her day, but there's always a first time for everything.

"Hi, Daddy," I say. I don't really want to talk to him, but I guess I should be nice because it's my birthday and all.

"Hey there, girl," he says nervously into my cell. We haven't spoken since I left the bucket he calls my first car in his driveway a couple months ago. "Happy birthday. How old are you now, sixteen?" he jokingly asks, but I know he's serious.

"Seventeen," I say. How could he forget how old his youngest daughter is? And, more importantly, how could he forget that my sweet-sixteenth birthday was last year? Maybe because, like all my birthdays, it wasn't that sweet or memorable because my former best friend from my old school, Family Christian, and I got busted shoplifting. Actually, I got busted while she was shoplifting and stuffed some boxer shorts into my backpack. Now I can never show my face again at the Ross in the O.C.—like I'd ever go in there again anyway.

"Okay, seventeen," he says defensively. As I take my backpack and purse out of my mom's car, there's an uncomfortable pause on the phone. "How's everything else going?"

"Everything's going fine, Daddy. I just got to school," I say, arming my car and heading toward the front gate. I purposely arrived early to campus this morning so I could get a good parking spot. There are barely any cars here yet, and it's quiet except for the squawking seagulls circling in the cloudy sky above my head.

"Oh, that's right. It is a school day," he says. "I just wanted to wish you a happy birthday and let you know your card's in the mail. Bye, baby." I hope there's a check accompanying the card when it arrives. With him, there's no telling.

"Thanks, Daddy, and have a good day," I say, flipping my phone closed and returning it to its pocket inside my purse. Talking to my father is always like pulling teeth.

"Happy birthday, bitch," Misty says, surprising me as I make my way from the main parking lot onto campus. What's she doing here so early, and why is she talking to me? Some people never learn their lesson, no matter how hard they fall in the process.

"I'm actually glad to see you this morning, and thanks for the greeting," I say, stepping up to her so close I can smell the cherry lip balm smeared all over her mouth. "I'm going to tell you for the last time, Misty. Back the hell up off me and my friends, or you'll be sorry."

"Your threats don't scare me," she says, taking a step so close, we're basically breathing for each other. Even with her heels on, we're still eye level. Looking at Misty has always been a little like looking in a warped mirror.

"They should," I say. Not backing down from her advance, my mind involuntarily cools, and my eyes begin to glow in hers. My mom's powers couldn't have manifested at a more perfect time, or so I think.

Careful, Jayd. You could catch a head cold, Misty says in her mind, and I suddenly feel my vision becoming cloudy. Oh hell no, she didn't use my own powers against me again. The warning bell rings, and the crowd of students starts flowing in from all directions, shutting down my vision quest for the time being, but my head feels congested. Misty smiles at her work as she walks away. What the hell just happened here? I don't have time to figure it out before first period, but she's not going to get away with her shit for much longer.

Spanish class was uneventful and busy, as usual. I wonder if Mr. Adewale ever gets tired of being on point all the time. I know I get tired of trying. We have a sample exam in English class this period, and after dealing with Misty's ass first thing this morning, I'm not feeling so good. I just want to go home and get in the bed. I can't deal with Mickey today, or anyone else for that matter. I need to find out what Misty's up to and fast if I'm going to fix this shit.

"Happy birthday, Jayd!" Alia and the rest of our AP crew say to me as I step into Mrs. Malone's room. Alia is holding a small ice cream cake from Baskin-Robbins, just like I said I wanted at last night's session when they asked me what I was doing for my birthday. I've been asking for it all month but didn't think anyone was listening. How is it that my associates heard what my best friends missed—or, more likely, ignored?

"Atchoo!" I sneeze loudly, unable to hold it in. "Sorry about that, and thank you," I say, slightly embarrassed at all the eyes on me, including Jeremy's. I bet this was all his doing.

"Well, don't just stand there," Mrs. Malone says. "Blow out the candles so we can get started." I follow her directions, blowing out all seventeen of the white candles, almost in tears by the time the last flame flickers out. This is the sweetest surprise ever.

"Here. I thought you might like a day to yourself," Jeremy says, handing me a big silver envelope. I carefully remove the gold ribbon holding it together, reading the red words on the white paper. What else could he possibly give me that he hasn't already?

"Oh, Jeremy," I say, reading the gift certificate for a full day of pampering at a spa. "I don't know what to say."

"How about thank you?" he says, looking at me strangely. "Are you feeling okay?"

"Actually, no," I say, sniffling a bit. "I think I'm coming down with something, but I'll be fine." The rest of the students sit down as Mrs. Malone returns to her desk.

"I'll see you at break," Jeremy says, kissing me on the forehead before walking out of our class to join his own.

"That reminds me," Mrs. Malone says, handing our exams to Charlotte, who dutifully passes them out to the rest of us, "Mrs. Bennett's absent today, so our meetings are canceled." That news alone is enough to make me feel better. Now if I could only get over whatever this is Misty has thrown my way, I'd be set for the rest of the day.

Just like I thought, Nellie and Mickey both forgot about my day. Mickey may have remembered, but as she's still not speaking to me, I guess I'll never know. And because Nigel's not talking to her, they're both in a foul mood, and I'm not reminding anyone to greet me during our ASU meeting. It's bad enough I had to sit through fourth period with them, waiting for some sort of acknowledgment, but I give up.

"Here, have a doughnut," Jeremy says, passing me a glazed treat. I'm going to be so high off sugar by the time the day is over, I won't know what to do with myself. On top of this morning's cake and ice cream, Jeremy surprised me again at break with flowers and balloons attached to a pound of my favorite See's candy. If I'd known how fond of birthdays Jeremy is, I would've had mine a long time ago.

"Who brought them?" I ask, biting into the sweet Krispy Kreme treats. One of these is as addictive as taking a hit off a crack pipe, I assume. Maybe we should give these to Pam, the resident crackhead on the block Mama feeds on the regular, instead of a hot plate. Pam might find another addiction and gain some weight at the same time, killing two birds with one stone.

"I don't know, but I say we have these at every meeting," Nigel says, licking the icing off his fingers as Mickey grabs two more doughnuts out of one of the three boxes stacked on Mr. A's desk. When he returns, the meeting will officially begin.

"Oh, did you want one?" Mickey asks Nigel, who looks amazed by how much his girl can put away. He shakes his head, and she continues eating, unashamed of the pounds she's packing on. There's still much tension in the air between them, but I can tell it's slowly dissipating, unlike the iceberg between Mickey and me. I'll let her completely chill the hell out before attempting to make nice. Besides, this shit is all her fault, as usual, and this time I refuse to be the first to speak.

"Enjoying the treats?" Misty asks, walking through the open door. A cold draft seems to follow her, reminding me of my dream about falling on black ice; that should be Misty's nickname because she's just as slick and dangerous as the real thing. "They're courtesy of KJ's campaign," she says. I stop eating the soft pastry in midbite, now knowing their mysterious origin. Oh shit, this can't be good for me.

"You bought these?" Mickey asks, chomping away on her third doughnut. "Thanks, I guess." That's the nicest thing Mickey has said to Misty in a long, long time. What did she put on these, and how do I protect myself from them? I knew I should've worn my bangles today. Something told me to gird my spiritual loins, but I didn't follow my first mind, and because I woke up at my mom's, Mama wasn't there to remind me like she would've done, had I been at home.

"Okay, students. Let's hear about how everyone's campaign is going," Mr. Adewale says, walking into the room. "Ms. Toni won't be joining us this afternoon, but she did move to hold the official vote after spring break in a couple weeks.

Any objections?" Not to that, but I think it should be illegal to bring food if you're intrinsically evil—I'll keep that suggestion to myself for the time being. I wrap the partially eaten pastry in a napkin and put it inside my purse. I'll have Mama take a look at it to see if my paranoia's running wild or if this girl really did put something in these.

"Man, I'm ready to vote now," Del says, smacking on the sugary twist in his hand. "KJ's the man for the job—no offense, Jayd."

"None taken, Del," I manage to say, but the room has seemingly dropped in temperature. "Is it just me, or did someone turn up the air conditioner?" I zip up my jacket and rub my arms, trying to warm myself up. So much for showing off my new bebe top and pants, courtesy of Jeremy.

"I think it's just you. I hope you didn't catch a cold; that's why I was out for the past two days," Misty says, her blue contacts gleaming. "Maybe your blood sugar's just low. Why don't you have another doughnut? It might help." She gestures to the pile of tainted sweets. She's not as slick with her shit as she thinks she is. Whatever Misty did is having an effect on me, but no one else seems to see what I see, which is no surprise.

"Yeah, I say we get this vote over with now," Nigel says, washing his snack down with water. "I'm ready." Something tells me if he voted now, it wouldn't be for me, even if he is my unofficial campaign manager. Mr. Adewale looks at me still shivering and at his desk where the doughnuts are. Before he can add it all up, Chance walks into the room with an armful of pizza boxes and balloons.

"What's this all about?" Mr. A asks, taking a few of the boxes from him and setting them down on top of an empty student desk.

"It's Jayd's birthday, Mr. A," Chance says, putting down the rest of the food and handing me more balloons before kissing me on the cheek. Mickey and Nellie look completely surprised by the news, but Nigel smiles. I knew he couldn't have forgotten about me, just like Rah—even if I don't expect to hear from him anytime soon after Mickey's confession. "This is from me and Nigel, girl."

"Happy birthday, Jayd," Mr. A says, walking over to give me a hug. Instead of feeling happy at his warm embrace, I feel sick to my stomach.

"I think I'm going to be sick," I say, running from the classroom, barely making it outside before chucking up the half doughnut and everything else in my stomach.

"Jayd!" Jeremy says, running after me. He grabs my hair, holding it out of the way, and I'm glad for it. There's nothing like getting vomit in my hair. I take a couple napkins from Mr. Adewale, who has joined us outside, and wipe my mouth dry. This is so uncute.

"Maybe you should go home and get some rest. I hear there's been a bug going around," Mr. Adewale says, walking back inside his room. He writes me a note to the office while Chance grabs all my birthday stuff, my purse, and my backpack.

"Come on, babe. I'll take you home," Jeremy says, pulling me up from my bent-over stance outside the door. Students walking by during the lunch hour look at me, pointing in disgust, and I can't say that I blame them. I know the rumors of me being pregnant or having a hangover will be flying around campus in no time.

"I'm sorry about that," I say, looking at the mess I've made. The whole group is watching from inside, but it's Misty's eyes I see. She doesn't look as happy as she did when I first took the doughnut. Maybe me getting ill was a good thing. I'll have to look up what I can in my mom's limited spirit notebook, but right now, I just want to get out of here, and it looks like my man is going to make my final birthday wish come true. I can't afford to be down for too long. With my exams, the speech, my spirit work, and money to be made, I don't have any time to lose. And more than that, I'm not letting Misty make me sick again. Like Mama says, fool me once, shame on you. Fool me twice, your ass is mine.

~ 10 ~
The Prodigal Daughter

"If he could move through the rumors, he could drive off of fumes."

—Kanye West

"*H*ere, have some tea," Maman says to me, passing me the delicate china cup and saucer. Bringing the spicy liquid to my lips, I try to take a sip, but the hot sting stops me before I can get a good taste.

"Ouch!" I say, backing away from our teatime.

"Careful not to burn yourself, Jayd," Maman says. She is dressed in delicate lace clothing that is almost completely translucent in the light, as is the rest of her body. We are in the same dark room in which I wrote in the spirit book and promptly fell on my behind when leaving another dream. But instead of sitting at the desk, we are seated on a fainting couch with a small coffee table in front of us. "Here, like this," she says, lifting the precious china teacup from the silver tray and raising it in demonstration. Pursing her lips carefully against the gold-trimmed edge, she quietly blows the top of the cup before sipping, instantly turning it into iced tea with her cool breath. "See, Jayd. If you take your time, you won't get hurt." I have a feeling she's talking about more than the drink I'm holding.

"Thank you, Maman." I follow Maman's example, which has the same effect on my portion. She's right: now that it's cooled off, it doesn't hurt at all.

"*A lady always takes her time in every situation,*" *Maman says, returning her cup to the tray and pouring another serving. "The tea will be just as sweet if you sip it slowly." She then takes one teaspoon of honey from the bowl next to the teapot, slowly stirring the thick gold sweetener until it completely immerses itself in the brown elixir.* I'm still getting used to the first cup. Even with the cooler temperature, it's full of bitter roots and spicy powders that make me gag. How Maman's taking cupfuls to the head is beyond me. "*The tea will be even sweeter if you slow down, because you can actually savor the entire body, not just the flavor, which makes the benefits last longer,*" *she says, tasting it again as if for the first time.*

"*Atchoo!*" I sneeze, wasting the cold liquid all over the couch and Maman's dress, but she doesn't react. Instead she continues drinking her tonic while I take one of the cloth napkins on the coffee table and pat her down.

"*Bless you, my child,*" *Maman says, touching my left hand with her right, stopping my movement. "Bless you.*" I look up at a smiling Maman, her jade eyes glowing. Maman's long gray hair seems to move like snakes around her neck, slithering slowly from her body to mine.

"*Maman,*" I plead. I've always been afraid of snakes, like most sane people I know. The cold-blooded reptiles slide up my arm and merge with my hair, which is hanging loosely around my shoulders. By the time they reach my scalp, I am no longer afraid. It feels kind of good to have Maman's hair in mine. The snakes massage my temples and then the rest of my head, soothing away my congestion with each vibration. What the hell was in that tea?

"Jayd, phone," Jeremy says, shaking me awake. I open my eyes, searching for the small cell near my head, half expecting snakes to grab it for me.

"*You better come correct how you approaching me. Rec-*

ognize a real woman," Keri Hilson sings, announcing the end of my dream and the last day of the school week, hallelujah. I'm feeling much better after staying home from school yesterday. I took the opportunity to look through my mom's spirit notes and found out that any time she would catch a cold is more than likely because she invaded a sick person's mind. There was also one story about how Esmeralda gave her a head cold with one look. I have a feeling that's exactly what Misty did, thanks to her godmother's old tricks.

I had to call Mama and tell her I wouldn't be able to make it to work yesterday, and of course she immediately could tell something was wrong. She gave me a special tea to brew, and it cleared most of my congestion and nausea right up. No one can match her hot toddies. It also gave me more vivid dreams than usual, like the one I just woke up from about Maman. Thankfully, there were no snakes in Mama's recipe. I even gave Jeremy a little bit just in case my virus was contagious. Even with my runny nose, Jeremy was still all over me, and I didn't mind one bit, once I felt better. Since my ugly episode at school on Wednesday, Jeremy hasn't left my side, making me soup, taking my temperature—the whole nine yards. Even if he never told me he loves me, I would definitely know it from Jeremy's actions. The boy is sprung, and I'm bouncing right along with him.

I don't know exactly what time Jeremy and I finally passed out, but we make great study partners. I still can't believe he stayed up all night with me, twice in a row. He also helped me make flash cards and then quizzed me with them. I'm going to be so ready for my Spanish and economics AP exams, but English is another story. It's been nice spending so much time with Jeremy. He's been spoiling me since I moved to Inglewood. If I knew life could be this good with a boyfriend, I would've moved to my mom's a long time ago.

"Aren't you glad you took a night off from the study

group?" Jeremy asks, kissing my eyebrows and then my cheeks. We both have morning breath but could not care less. I snatch up my phone and silence the ringing alarm. We both had better get going before we're late for school. I already took yesterday off, per Mama's request after I told her about the instant coldlike symptoms due to my encounter with Misty on Wednesday and the mysterious doughnuts she brought to the meeting. Because of Mama's prescription, I feel much better, but still not one hundred percent.

"Yes, and in more ways than one," I say, rising from our makeshift cot on the living room floor. My mom's couch can fit only me comfortably. Sometimes I need space, especially with the baked beans I finished off from the leftovers last night. A sistah's only human. "All that expensive tea is putting a damper on my funds." I need to go to the market today and stock up the refrigerator for next week. I never knew it was so expensive to feed myself for every single meal, not that I have much variety in my diet these days. Unlike Mama, I have yet to master the art of cooking various meals. It will be mostly grilled cheese and soup for me from now on.

"Do you need some cash?" Jeremy asks, following me up. "I can spot you until your next pay day." I need one of those and bad. I've been taking way too much time off work at Netta's and with my own clients. It's hurting my pockets and their heads. I saw Shawntrese yesterday, and she was sporting a cap for the third day in a row. I've got to get back on my game. I'm ultimately hurting myself, and that definitely won't make me feel any better.

"You're sweet, baby, but I'll be okay." Jeremy can't help wanting to bail me out, and I'm learning to appreciate it. Against my wishes, he reaches for his wallet and pulls out a twenty.

"Here. This should cover my munchies for the last two

nights and a down payment for next time." Before I can say anything else, he kisses me, silencing me for the moment.

"I'd better get going," he says, kissing me one more time on the nose before putting on his worn tan Birkenstocks and claiming his hoodie from the coatrack. "Next time I'll bring a change of clothes."

"Okay," I say, following Jeremy to the door. He bends down and kisses me on the forehead, hugging me tightly.

"See you at school," Jeremy says, unlocking the front door and letting himself out. After he's gone, I lie back down for a moment. I can't believe I'm regularly spending the night with a boy other than Rah. Both dudes have never pressured me about having sex, and for that I'm grateful. Just being with Jeremy makes me happier than I've been in a long, long time. And the fact that he's so helpful is such a bonus. I'd better count my blessings now before they vanish into thin air like everything else that brings me joy. Now it's time to face my Friday and get to South Bay High before the time slips away, too.

The morning chill is more pronounced from Inglewood to Redondo Beach than from Compton because the drive to school is along the coast, going through El Segundo, Manhattan Beach, and Hermosa Beach, finally making it down Pacific Coast Highway and into Redondo. It would be a nice view this morning if the fog weren't so thick. Today I'm taking my time getting to campus. The last time I arrived early, I ran into Misty, and I definitely don't want to make that mistake again. My immune system can't take another dose of her poison just yet. Because of the heffa, my birthday took a foul turn, but when I make a full recovery, Misty's first on my shit list. Second is Rah, who didn't even call to wish me happy birthday, but I say "whatever" to his trifling ass, too. In order to get through these next few weeks, I'm going to pretend like all my haters are invisible; I've got too much to do to let their bull keep me down.

Even though it's Friday, we still have a study session this evening, and I haven't even begun writing my speech for Sunday's sermon. I have to work at Netta's after school, so I'll make it only to the tail end of the session—but I will make it, unlike last night. Jeremy and I got a lot of studying done, but we also played, which I know will not be the case at Charlotte's house. There's nothing fun about that girl, and because of her uptight ass, I must say I'm impressed with my academic prowess since joining the group. I can't wait to tell Ms. Toni about my progress and to see about checking out another book from her personal library for the break next week. But before I can make it down the main hall to see if my school mama's in her office, I notice my crew by Mickey's locker, and they don't look like they're talking about the weather.

"What's up?" I ask Chance. Nellie shakes her head, indicating that this isn't the time for small talk. Ever since Nigel found out that Mickey had another man on the side besides her ex-man before she got pregnant, his temper has been a bit sensitive, to say the least. I guess Nigel's ego can't handle being one of two men Mickey was fooling around with before her man got locked up. What a mess.

"Mickey, what the hell is this all about?" Nigel asks, waving an envelope in the air.

"It's nothing, Nigel. Give it back to me," Mickey says, reaching for the letter, but it's too late. Nigel notices the numbers on the envelope and knows it's from an inmate at a penitentiary, even if he doesn't recognize the name in front of them. "You and your ex-man are pen pals now, Mickey? After all that nigga did?"

"It's not like that," she says, reaching for the paper, but, again, it's no use. Her swollen belly won't let her move too quickly these days. Nigel rips the letter out of its envelope and quickly reads part of it.

"Really? Then what is it like, because it sounds like he's planning a future with you and your baby, which apparently isn't his either? How many niggas have you been with in the past six months, huh, Mickey?" We all stop and stare at Nigel, who has lost all remnants of any type of control. I wish I could help cool him off before he says something he will regret, but we're past that point.

"Come on, man. Back off," Chance says, putting his left hand on Nigel's shoulder, but I doubt Nigel can feel a thing. He's too pumped up off anger to listen to reason. I'd better send Rah a text that his boy's about to blow. He'll be up here in less than the twenty minutes it normally takes to get from his school to ours. Westingle High is near LAX, and Rah knows several ways to get to and from there and here. One day when we're speaking again I'm going to have him give me directions because I know of only one route other than taking the freeway, which is rarely an option because there's always traffic on the 405.

"He almost shot me, Mickey," Nigel says, almost in tears. "And he killed Tre. I went to school with that nigga and now he's dead." Mickey looks at us, horrified at the embarrassing truth. "How could you betray me like that?" Maybe now she'll finally learn her lesson.

"Nigel, I'm sorry," Mickey says, trying to wipe the saltwater flowing freely from Nigel's face with her hands, but he grabs them both, stopping her in midair.

"Don't ever touch me again. I'm through with you until you have a paternity test," Nigel says, forcing her hands down. "My mother was right about you," he adds as tears stream down Mickey's face, causing her MAC foundation to smear. "You're a straight-up gold-digging ho."

"Nigel, no! Please!" Mickey screams after him, but he's already out of the main hall and on his way to fourth period like the rest of us should be. The other students stare at a hysterical Mickey as she falls into Nellie's arms. Misty and KJ catch the end of the argument but see enough to make them smile.

"He just needs some air," Nellie says, holding our girl. I want to help, but Mickey's so hurt she'll need someone to blame, and I'm already carrying enough of her misplaced anger. I did my part by alerting Rah, who I know is already on his way. There's nothing more I can do for my girl or her baby, who is my main concern. I hope they can fix this mess, but it doesn't look good from where I or the other fifty or so witnesses are standing.

"We'd better get to class," Chance says, noticing the hall emptying quickly, and he's right. There's nothing more to see here. We're all on our way to fourth period, but I hope this doesn't continue in class. It might be speech and debate, but Mickey's sex life is not a topic for public discussion.

"Are we ready for our exam on the basic rules of forensic debate and engaging your opponent?" Mr. Adewale asks the class as he passes out our test sheets, reminding me of our study session tonight. I can't believe the Advanced Placement exams are less than a month away. I feel better about my progress, but I'm nowhere near ready.

"Ah, Mr. Adewale—I thought we'd get a break this week," Del says from the back of the classroom where he and the rest of the South Central members congregate. Emilio passes out the rest of the sheets while Mr. A goes back to his desk to set the timer, ignoring the rude outburst. We get only forty minutes to finish and then will spend the last ten minutes of the class period grading our tests.

"This is a closed-book exam, Miss Caldwell," Mr. A says to

Misty, who gives him the evil eye, but her tricks won't work on him. She doesn't know that Mr. Adewale is also a priest in our religion, and I think he should keep it that way for as long as possible. Knowing Misty's sneaky ass, she'll figure out a way to use his gifts to her advantage like she's done with me.

"But, Mr. Adewale, that's not fair. I didn't have a chance to study or anything, and it's Friday," Misty whines. She's gotten real good at using her new look to get what she wants from the dudes, but Mr. A isn't the average man. Completely pissed, Misty reluctantly places her textbook on the floor next to her backpack and rolls her blue eyes sky high. She's a hot mess if there ever was one. Mr. Adewale looks at Misty, shakes his head, and continues with his lesson plan. That's one advantage to being in AP classes—they teach you to read ahead because the teacher may drop a quiz at any given moment like Mr. A is doing. If Misty would worry more about her own shit instead of always being up in mine and everybody else's, maybe she'd get more studying done.

"Glad to see you're feeling better, Miss Jackson," Mr. Adewale says, smiling at me and me at him. His charm never wears thin on me. "Let's get to it." I can see the rest of the class is unimpressed with our young teacher, including Jeremy. He's always been slightly jealous of my bond with Mr. A, but I hope we're over that. I can't have him mad at me while my friends are tripping, too. As we all get ready to turn over our test questions, Rah steps through the open door, sparing us all a few more moments from the inevitable.

"Excuse me, Mr. Adewale. I just came to check on Nigel," Rah says, handing our teacher his office pass. Nigel put Rah down as his brother, and the administration never questions Rah when he comes up here. They've had more family-emergency excuses than anyone I know, not that Rah would need to use them with Mr. Adewale. They've been cool since Mr. A refereed a basketball game between Rah and our boys, and KJ and his boys at the beginning of the school year.

"Is everything okay, Nigel?" Mr. A asks, noticing the tense vibe between Nigel and Mickey, who is seated next to her man in their usual spot.

"Yeah, man," Nigel says, standing up. "I just need to clear my head for a minute, if that's cool."

"Nah, that ain't cool," KJ says, waving his hand and shaking his head. "You ain't special because you can't control your woman. I can help you with that later, dog." KJ and his boys get a good laugh at a very serious situation that Nigel finds anything but amusing.

"Man, you need to shut the hell up before I do it for you."

KJ stops laughing at the seriousness in my boy's tone and the blank look in his eyes. We all know that stare. When Nigel's on the football field, he gets that same exact glare when he's about to take down any dude foolish enough to get in his way, but Misty apparently didn't get the memo.

"It's just the truth—it ain't fair."

Why is Misty talking? Nobody asked her opinion. See what I'm saying—if she'd mind her own business, she'd get a lot further in life. Misty looks across the room and into my eyes, but little does she know her trick didn't have a lasting effect on me. My mom's gift moves in, my vision becoming hers, and it's not a good feeling. There's nothing but confusion in Misty's head. I can't make out one thought from the other and feel drained after being in here for only a second.

"I need to get out of here," Nigel says, stating my thoughts exactly before grabbing his bag from the floor and hitting Mickey's foot trying to make his escape. Mickey looks up at her man's hard scowl and completely breaks down.

"It's Tre's baby, okay, Nigel!" Mickey yells, shutting everybody up with her confession. Misty and I look away from each other and at the *Jerry Springer* scene unfolding before us. "You're right, I'm nothing but a ho. Are you happy now?" Mickey storms out of the room, running into Rah on her way out. Damn, I wasn't expecting that one. Talk about the shit hitting the fan. Nellie runs after our girl, and I stay seated, waiting to see how it's all going to end. Jeremy looks like the rest of the white students in the classroom: completely amazed. Without another word, Mr. A writes Nigel a pass, and he and Rah leave us to our test. Mr. Adewale may be cool, but business is business. I could learn a lot by adopting the same philosophy when it comes to separating drama from the really important stuff, like this test in front of me. At the end of the day, there's not much I can do but pray that Nigel forgives Mickey for her indiscretions and lets her back into his heart, and that's exactly what I'm going to do. In the meantime, I'm going to handle my business because I've got a full day and night ahead of me.

I was so tired when I got in last night I fell down on my mom's couch in my clothes. It was the second night I have spent alone since I moved in here a week ago. If it weren't for the late-night study session after working at Netta's, I probably wouldn't have slept as good as I did. Mama's coming around little by little, mostly because she can't stay mad at me when I'm sick. When I'm not feeling well, healing me outweighs everything else.

I look forward to the study sessions like a regular night hanging out with a group of friends. Even Charlotte's not so bad once I got to know her. She even had cake with the rest of our English class on my birthday, and I thought that was pretty big of her. Maybe she's not such a hater after all—unlike Misty, who can't help herself, but, lucky for me, I'm learning how to handle her insanity. When I got a glimpse of her thoughts yesterday, I could see that Misty doesn't know which way is which—literally. She thinks being sneaky and manipulative is the only way to get what she wants, but what that is exactly is still a mystery to me. And from what little I could see, it's a mystery to Misty, too.

No matter what Misty does, I always end up wanting to help her after I get my payback. I found a story called *The Prodigal Daughter* in my mother's notebook, which she copied from the spirit book. It might help me help this trick so I can help my friends, too. It seems that everywhere Misty goes, she causes trouble, feeding off the negative energy she can create. It's almost as if her head is calm only when there's chaos around her. If I could find another outlet for Misty to direct her energy, maybe she'd be happy and think clearly— ultimately having a cool head rest on her shoulders. I just want to help Misty achieve that thought process more quickly, and my mom's story may help me do just that.

When my mother lost her gift of sight, Mama made her write the story down in the spirit book as a warning tale without naming the prodigal child. She is referred to only as "the woman with the hot head," like in the odu, the divine stories of different events in the lives of orisha. But my mom's tragedy is more of an ode to a lost portion of our legacy than a lesson on righteous character. My mom lost her powers, and Mama has always wished they would return to the bloodline one day. I think the ancestors have answered Mama's call. Through my dreams, the prodigal daughter has returned.

In light of this new development, I am convinced I have to keep my mom's powers a secret. If I learn how to use them effectively, Mama will be so happy about the power being back in our possession that she'll forgive my defiant behavior, I hope. The only thing she said to me yesterday was that we were having brunch with my mom and Netta after church on Sunday. That was her way of telling me that, yes, she's coming to the sermon and that she and my mom have come to a compromise regarding the traditional celebration of our birthdays, which makes part of my job easy. The incantation for the return of the prodigal daughter to the household is for the mother and child to break bread together after I say the chant. I've been working it into my speech all afternoon. My last client left about two hours ago, and I have been sitting at the dining room table writing ever since.

I need a break, but my boo is helping Chance do some work on his car this evening. It's been too long since I had a night all to myself, and I should take advantage of it. The responsible side of me says I have grocery shopping to do, but the other side tells me to drive to the Fox Hills Mall and get a Hot Dog on a Stick and chill for a while. It's not the best dinner, but it'll satisfy my craving, and it's only ten minutes away. I miss Mama's cooking and her company. I can't believe I'm thinking this, but I even miss all the spirit work I would help her do on a daily basis. After tomorrow's sweet words, hopefully I'll be able to kick it with Mama without so much pain between us.

As I pull into the parking lot in front of the mall, my phone vibrates. I pick it up from the passenger's seat and immediately open it to hear my man's voice. Since Mr. Adewale's smile at me in class yesterday, Jeremy's been more reserved than usual. He didn't even offer to come over last night. Maybe he just needed some space to gain perspective on his unfounded jealousy. Jeremy should know by now that he's got me like I've got him, and I'm not letting go anytime soon.

"Hey, Jeremy," I say, turning off my iPod and car. I look around at the other cars in the brightly lit covered lot, scoping my surroundings. A girl can't be too careful when she's alone.

"Hey, baby. What are you up to?" Jeremy asks. I love it when he checks up on me.

"I just got to the mall, about to hang out for a little while, enjoy some me time. What are you doing?" My mother's dark tinted windows allow me privacy to finish my conversation before I get out and join the rest of the shoppers. Nothing irks me more than when someone is engaged in a full-blown phone conversation in public.

"Chance and I are at the pier off First and Main with some friends. It's pretty cool," he says. I can hear a girl's laughter in the background, and it's not Nellie. What kind of friends are we talking about?

"Do they have anything to eat?" I ask, restarting my engine and heading in his direction.

"Yeah, there's plenty of food here. They even have pretzels, your favorite." I can hear Jeremy's smile through the phone. "I'll see you later, babe. We're about to go into a dead spot." He breaks up because of the bad connection.

"Okay, baby." The Santa Monica Pier isn't that big, so it should be easy to find them. Besides, if I know my man, he's found a spot to post up, and I'm on my way to relax with him.

Unlike the mall, parking by the beach is limited and costs money. The pier is packed tonight with mostly couples. It's the perfect affordable, romantic date place. As I predicted, Jeremy and Chance are seated at one of the picnic tables along the path with Alia and Candace from our AP group. If I didn't know better, I'd say they were on a date like the other people around us. Making my way down the trail toward their table, I can see them getting up to leave, walking in the opposite direction. I'd better quicken my pace if I want to catch up to them. I tried calling Jeremy, but it kept going to voice mail. I guess he really doesn't get a signal out here.

"Hey, Jeremy," I say, walking up behind him and putting my arms around his waist. Chance, Candace, and Alia look up, shocked to see me. Didn't they know I was coming?

"Jayd, I thought you were at the mall. What are you doing here?" Jeremy asks, turning around to face me. He looks like he's just been caught cheating, and that's what it feels like, too. But that doesn't make any sense. Players don't give up their rendezvous locations.

"Why would you tell me where you were if you didn't want me to come?" I ask, pissed as all get-out. I feel completely uncomfortable and insecure, and Candace's guilty look isn't helping much.

"I was just talking. I didn't think you'd actually change your plans and come all the way down here." Jeremy looks at Candace and Alia and then back down at me. I know he can see what I see so clearly: he's busted.

"Sorry, but my psychic wi-fi is off right now, just like your phone, I guess. I don't know what you were thinking when you called me while you were on a date. I'm out of here." I turn around and head back toward my car. He can have his date, and if Chance thinks I'm not telling Nellie, he's got another think coming.

"But, Jayd . . ." Jeremy begins, but I don't want to hear it. I've been through this type of madness with Rah too many times to count, and I'll be damned if I make that same mistake in this relationship. "It's not like that. And I didn't tell you to come because you said you were busy." Did I just hear him right? Is he denying the conversation we had less than fifteen minutes ago?

"I know I heard you right when you basically told me to change my plans and come over here. And now I get here, parking paid for, and you're leaving with a girl nonetheless? What the hell, Jeremy?" If this is a simple misunderstanding, Jeremy had better learn how to communicate properly with a black woman, and fast, if he's going to be with me.

"We were putting money in the meters," Chance says, pointing to their cars parked on the street behind us.

"Okay, this is one of those hissy fits that's actually your rational reaction to a simple misunderstanding, right?" Jeremy asks, almost reading my mind verbatim. If he were smiling, I'd think he was trying to be a smart-ass, but I think he's actually sincere in his quest for understanding. I wish I could jump into Jeremy's mind right now, but my head's too hot.

"Are you being serious or patronizing? Because I can't tell," I say as Alia smiles at our scene. Chance looks behind him to make sure his car is okay, new rims and all. Boys and their toys, I swear. I understand because the wheels do look flyy, but still.

"Jayd, I told you I'm always on your side, but sometimes you make me out to be the enemy just because that's what you're used to, and that's not fair to me or to us." Maybe Jeremy does have a valid point. Sometimes I'm so used to having issues with boys I don't know how to act in a normal relationship, if that's what this is.

"Jeremy, please tell me you didn't invite me to come over here and hang out with you and Chance," I ask, embarrassed that I let my emotions get the best of me, but I know what I heard. And Jeremy should know what he implied even if he didn't fully say it.

"I didn't, not really, but I can see how you'd react to seeing me leave with another girl. It doesn't feel good being jealous, does it?" Jeremy asks, taking me by the waist and kissing my lips, forcing me to smile. "I'm sorry I wasn't clearer, Jayd. But we can still save the evening, if you want." He takes my hand in his, raising it to his lips and kissing my knuckles. He sure does know how to calm a sistah down.

"I think you two are the sweetest thing ever," Alia says, looking dead at Chance as she says it. Alia's had a crush on Chance since I've known them both, and I think it goes back to their days in elementary school. Nellie better watch herself. If she turns into the white girl she's going for, she just might drive her man away from the black girl we all know and love. Why have a wannabe when you can have the real thing?

"So what are we doing?" I ask, surrendering to the moment. Forgiveness is the most important element in any good relationship, and I'm choosing to practice it often when it comes to the people who matter most in my life. Maybe Candace will get the message and back up off my man, because I know she's digging him.

"The night is young," Chance says, walking toward his Nova with Alia on one arm and Candace on the other. Should I warn Nellie that her bougie friends are distracting her from her man? Maybe later, but right now I just want to get something in my stomach. I'll worry about mending relationships tomorrow.

By the time I got in last night from hanging with my friends, it was too late to try to memorize my speech. Instead I put it on note cards when I got up this morning, but I'll probably end up winging most of it. The church is packed with young people for the special services planned all day to cater to the teen-and-under crowd. It's five after eleven, and my mom's still not here. I know she's not into church—especially not her father's church—but I figured she'd show up for my first public speech. I really wanted her to be here for this. But it looks like my words will have to work their magic on Mama. I hope the residuals will hit my mom if she does decide to show up late.

I hate that my two moms are fighting, and I feel like it's mostly my fault. I mean, their feud has been going on since my mother learned how to talk, but my moving out didn't help matters much. I'm going to change all that when it's my turn at the mic. My congestion isn't fully gone yet, but my head is clearer than it's been in a long time.

"Jayd, are you ready? After the choir sings, you're up," Daddy whispers to me from his great seat. I'm seated next to him, like I'm the first lady of the church. When Mama stepped down, her equally adorned but slightly smaller seat became the guest chair. When there are no guests, the seat remains empty, a constant reminder that no one can ever take Mama's place in the church—or anywhere else, for that matter.

"Yes, Daddy, I'm ready," I say, shaking slightly. I guess this is what they call having cold feet. I've never been this nervous before. I look down at my index cards, praying for my mother to walk through the door. I need for her to be here when I make my speech. My mom's notes said all parties have to hear the words simultaneously, or the spell won't work. We also have to break bread together soon after for it to seal. Where is she?

I'm right here, Jayd, my mom says, creeping into my thoughts right as the choir sings the last note of one of my favorite gospel songs. I was about to weep like Mary in the song if my mom didn't at least check in.

Mom, where are you? Daddy's introducing me now, I think back, half listening to my grandfather share his pride in me with the congregation. I'm just glad we're over the wench-calling part of our relationship. I never want Daddy to be mad at me like that again.

I'm sorry, baby, but I'm running a little late. I'm on my way, and I'll stay here the entire time so I can hear your speech as you say it, okay? That actually might work. It won't do anything to keep Mama from being even more pissed at her tardiness, but it should work for my ulterior motive.

Okay, but you'd better get here soon. Mama's calling you everything but a child of God, and in the Lord's house, too, I say telepathically, looking at Netta and Mama eye the room.

Mama can't help but glance back at the double doors leading into the main sanctuary from the front door, hoping to see my mother walk through at any moment. I wish I could inform her of my mother's impending arrival, but no such luck. I'm on.

"Thank you, Daddy, and good morning, church," I say, looking out into the crowd of over one hundred folks dressed in their Easter Sunday best. It's always a full house for the holidays.

"Good morning," the congregation replies. Here goes nothing.

"There are many types of returns. And I want to talk about bringing joy back to life and peace and harmony back home, starting with your own relationships, especially those between a mother and child." I check in with my mom to make sure she's listening, and she is. I've also got Mama's full attention, as well as the church members. I hope I don't lose them, because the speech I'm giving isn't going to be the typical Easter Sunday discourse.

"Amen, little sister," says one of the elder women seated in the first pew while waving a paper fan toward me, egging me on.

"Well." Another obligatory comment from the congregation floats through the now still air, waiting for me to continue.

"I can speak only for daughters because, well, that's what I am. But I suspect the same type of love and respect is due from son to mother, too." I hope Mama's really listening to my message this morning. Not only does she need to back up off us girls a bit, but she also needs to check her sons. This has been going on for two generations, and there's no time like the present to break this negative cycle once and for all.

"Preach! "shouts one of the female junior pastors from her

chair behind me. I haven't even gotten started yet, and they're already feeling me. I just hope it continues past what I'm about to say.

"And as a young woman, I look up to my mothers for being mothers. For constantly supporting me, taking care of me when I'm sick and sad, for rejoicing in my happiness with me, and for teaching me right from wrong, always." I look at Mama, who looks back at me, beaming with pride. Even if she was against me speaking at Daddy's church today, she was always for me showing off my oratory skills in front of our haters. Misty and her mom are here, too, minus Esmeralda. That woman knows better than to step in any building while Mama's inside, unless she wants to get beat down.

"But I also look to them to show me how to be a woman, how a woman interacts with the men in her life and other women as well. It seems like in my generation a lot of the mutual respect and adoration for one another as women is lost in the past."

"Yes, Lawd," the same junior pastor says from behind me. I guess she can relate. I can only imagine the hate she must get from the other sisters in the church, being the only female representative on the pulpit right now.

"Say it, little sistah," calls out another woman from the congregation. The choir even starts to hum, which is an indication that I'm definitely on point this morning. I can see why Daddy likes his job so much. There's a surge of power that comes with this post.

Okay, little girl. Don't get ahead of yourself, my mom interjects, checking the mini dictator in me. I'm glad she's still here listening.

"I don't know about y'all, but I'm tired of the drama between us girls," I say, looking directly into Misty's eyes. I try to enter her mind, but it's too cloudy for me to see. My words alone will have to reach her. "I'm tired of the evil eyes and gossip that's all too prevalent among girls my age and older women, too." As the holy ghost of truth roars through the small building like thunder, I notice one of Daddy's girl-friends look sideways at Mama. It's the same lady I saw Daddy talking to at the house a few weeks ago, and she also left the juju bag Mama had to fix. That woman's got her nerve plus some. She already had Mama go after her for bringing Daddy a cake, and now she's trying to give my grandmother the evil eye. Some people just don't learn.

"Let's bring back the spirit of love between us," I say. No matter what my cards say, apparently I'm done because the choir takes over, and so does the congregation with a standing ovation. Mama and Netta are crying, and so is my mom in my head. Even Misty looks slightly moved by my words. I guess my job here is done.

In the traditional fashion of any black church, a huge feast is underway for the after-church dinner. It looks delicious, but I already made plans at the Cheesecake Factory, and we need to get going if we're going to make our reservations, but Mama's got too many admirers to escape quietly.

"Sister James. So nice to see you again," the junior pastor says to Mama, who's looking for the quickest exit possible, but not before this woman sinks her claws into my grand-mother.

"It's nice to see you again, Pastor Trudy. You were in col-lege the last time I saw you, girl. You look good." Mama ac-cepts the sister's embrace before returning to her fanning. Daddy's church is good for advertising on the back of fans, sharing the paper-and-wood complimentary gift with the local funeral home's advertisement on the other side. It's a good reminder that the other side of life is death, and vice versa.

"Why, thank you, Sister James. And you haven't aged a

day," she says, eyeing Mama like a porkchop. What does this broad want with her? "And this one here is a special young lady," she says, patting me on the shoulder. Her touch reminds me of Mrs. Bennett's reptilian hands. She gives me the creeps.

"Yes, she is," Mama says, gently pulling my arm, forcing me away from our admirer and closer to where Netta and she are standing. Where is my mom? She should've been here by now. Finally, walking through the front door, the lost child returns to her father's church. My mom looks nervous but as fierce as usual, and everyone takes notice.

"What took you so long to get here, Lynn Marie, or have you forgotten what time church starts?" Mama asks my mom as she walks into the building against the tide. People are standing everywhere and talking up a storm, mostly about us.

"Traffic," my mom says. Netta and Mama roll their eyes at her obvious lie. There's not much traffic from Inglewood to Compton on a Sunday morning. "So are we having brunch or what? I'm starved," my mom says, looking and smelling like she just got out of the shower. More than likely she and Karl slept in late, and from the cross looks on Mama and Netta's faces, I'd say they're thinking the same thing.

"I bet," Mama says with a tone that's salty even for her.

"What's that supposed to mean?" my mom asks with one hand on her hip while the other holds her black Prada clutch tightly under her left arm. I can't wait to raid my mom's gifts, starting with her new purse. Her thigh-high black boots are making heads turn, and the tension between my mom and Mama also causes tongues to wag even faster. But before Mama can answer her daughter, the churchwomen throw in their two cents like they don't know who they're talking to.

"Maybe if her mama came back to the church on a regular basis, she'd know what to do and how to act, like the young sister said." Oh no, she didn't use my own words against

Mama. Who the hell does she think she is? This is a bold bunch of sisters. No wonder Misty's a regular member. She's their perfect protégé.

"And how to dress," one of her two friends says, looking my mother up and down like she just walked in off the street corner from turning tricks all night.

"Your husband seems to like my outfit just fine," my mom says, smiling wickedly at the woman's husband from his stance where he's salivating by the sanctuary door. Oh hell. It's about to get live up in this place, for real.

"Evil! All of you, just no-good hussies," the woman says, her friends pulling her away from my mom, Mama, and Netta. They already know they're no match for us.

"Is everything all right here?" Daddy asks, looking a little stressed and stepping out of the main sanctuary and into the social room where we're gathered. I guess having Mama and her girls back in the church was more than a notion.

"Yes, Daddy," I say, intervening before Mama gets to cussing everyone out, including him, just for the hell of it. "Thank you for having me speak today. It was real cool." Mama looks at my mom and sucks her teeth in disgust, and my mom promptly rolls her neck like a teenager. As far as I'm concerned, they both need to grow up. I don't come to church often, but I know this is neither the time nor the place for their beef.

"I'm the one who should be thanking you, Tweet. Maybe there's hope for you yet," he says, kissing me on the forehead.

"And what is that supposed to mean, Pastor James?" Mama interjects. "There's hope for the girl whether she speaks up in here or not." Why did he have to go say that in front of Mama? Is Daddy looking for more problems or what?

"You know exactly what I mean, Lynn Mae. This girl has a natural, God-given talent for preaching. I think she should come to church with me more often. She's my granddaughter, too, you know." Now Mama's really about to lose it. Where's a fire or some other catastrophic distraction when I need one?

"There's more than one way to skin a cat, or have you forgotten?" Mama asks between gritted teeth. Netta looks at her homegirl, recognizing that she's been pushed too far. I guess Daddy feels invincible in the house of his Lord, but he forgets Mama's power knows no boundaries. Church or not, she'll go off on him and everyone else up in here.

"No, I haven't, but I wish you would," Daddy says, hushing the attentive spectators. Mama looks around at his flock and then stares at him hard. He returns the action for as long as he can take it, eventually surrendering to Mama's view.

"Speaking of food, Lynn Mae, why don't we go on and get to the restaurant? You know it's going to be a long line if we wait any longer," Netta says, directing Mama away from the crowd. My mom's too busy texting whom I assume is Karl to care about the conversation going on between her parents. She's always been immune to their shit. I wish I could be so lucky.

"Mom, are you ready?" I ask, forcing her to focus on the moment in front of her. Ever since she got that ring on her finger, she's turned into a schoolgirl all over again. If this is how getting married makes a sistah act, I'm cool for the time being.

Before I can lead the way out, Misty catches my eye, and I feel a chill come over me like the last time she infected me. I suddenly feel light-headed. Why do I keep forgetting to wear my jade? Mama looks at Misty and breaks her hold on me with one glance. Thank God for Mama. What would I do without her always having my back?

"I knew it was a bad idea for you to be here," Mama says, catching me before I fall to the ground. Netta helps Mama keep me on my feet, steadily moving toward the front door. What the hell was that?

"My baby," my mom says, stroking my cheek.

"It was too soon after her cold for her to go out," Mama says, feeling my head with her hand, which feels like fire next to my skin. "Let's get her to Dr. Whitmore right now."

"No. I just need to eat," I say, barely able to stand up on my own. I've got to slap those contacts out of Misty's eyes once and for all. I can't take any more psychic hits like this one.

"Are you sure?" my mom asks, looking at me for some clue as to what's wrong with me. Her eyes look worried and filled with guilt. I hug her to communicate that this isn't her fault, and she hugs me back, much to Mama's disliking.

"She's probably been eating nothing but shit over at your place," Mama says, breaking our embrace and walking me out the door and down the front steps of the church. I doubt we'll be coming back here anytime soon. "We're going home to eat," she says, making the final decision.

"Sounds good to me," Netta says, helping my mom and grandmother walk me to the parking lot. The church ladies are really talking now, and I say let them. My only wish is that the Williams women stay tight like glue no matter what our haters do or say to try to bring us down. We're stronger than they'll ever know, and we will be here long after their lies are forgotten.

~ 11 ~
Sweet Revenge

*"I just wanna be/
I just wanna be successful."*

—DRAKE

Lexi greets Mama as she leads the way through the back gate, heading straight for the spirit room. I haven't been back here since I left, and my mom hasn't been in Compton since Christmas. It's ironic that she's returning on Easter. Mama's trying to fake the funk, but I know she's happy to have her girls home so she can make everything better. For Mama, that's all she needs to prove that she's right—about everything, all the time.

"I'll close the gate," Netta says, pushing the wooden doors shut as we walk past the garage and into the attached backhouse. When Mama unlocks the door it's quite evident that she and Netta have been busy in preparation for the bembé tonight. I'm supposed to join them, and I always look forward to the party signifying the end of an initiation, but I don't feel like going anywhere but straight to bed.

"Here, baby. Lie down on the mat," Mama says, rolling out the bamboo for me to rest. "Did you finish the round of tea I told you to make?"

"Yes, I did, and I followed your directions to the letter," I say, making myself comfortable on the floor. I grab one of the folded quilts in the corner next to my head and drape it across my body. It's a warm day outside, but it's cold in here to me. My mom sits down at the table as Netta and Mama buzz around her head like worker bees.

"Well, then, we'll have to see what else is going on then." That means Mama's going to give me a reading. So much for resting.

"I'll start cooking," Netta says, washing her hands in the sink. My mom's in a deep text conversation, probably making plans for this evening with her boo. I wish I was doing the same thing, but tonight was supposed to be about me helping Mama, giving Jeremy a night out without me. Because there's no school this week, we're spending every day studying and every night chilling, so the fact that he's hanging with his friends tonight is a good thing. He'd better act right and not hang out with any lonely girls, especially not Candace. I know she likes my man, but I'll have to deal with that later. Setting Misty straight is my top priority this afternoon.

"Lynn Marie, get your ass up and help Netta," Mama says, sitting down on the mat next to me. She opens the ancestor shrine in the opposite corner of the blankets and says a prayer. My mom and Netta stop what they're doing in respect for the chant. Mama takes a glass of water from the altar and her divination tray, pouring a libation to start the reading.

"You stay right there, baby," Mama says, placing her left hand on my head and mixing the sixteen cowries with her right. Finished with her Yoruba praises to the various orisha and our ancestors, Mama throws the shells with both hands, upset by the odu that falls on the woven tray.

"What is it, Mama?" I ask, scared of the alarmed look in her eyes. I've never seen a reading where all the cowries are facedown. That can't be a good sign.

"This letter is too hot to read," Mama says, scraping the odu off the mat with one swipe. After gathering the cowries, she dumps them in the glass of water, rising from the mat and covering the cup with her hand. Mama opens the screen door and tosses the water out through her fingers with the shells still inside the glass.

"What's really going on, Jayd?" Netta asks from her stance at the stove. She's found all the ingredients needed to make a slamming brunch, and my mom even looks excited to eat.

"It's too much to say." And that's all I'm willing to tell them. I'm positive that me holding on to my mom's sight is a good thing, as long as I can remember to wear my jade bracelets for protection against my enemies.

"Well, it's definitely a hot time in your life right now, and you need to cool off completely before you can make any real progress." I know Mama knows more than that, but she's not worried with sharing the details right now. I can tell by her concerned look that she just wants to rectify the situation at hand as quickly as possible, and so do I. "My little fire child," Mama says, replacing the cowries on the shrine.

"Have you been wearing your bracelets?" Netta asks.

"No," I say, ashamed of my forgetfulness. I'm too young to lose my memory. I think my mind has become cluttered with all the AP information and is keeping me off my spiritual guard.

Exactly, my mom thinks to me. *Don't be embarrassed, Jayd. We all forget things sometimes.*

"Well, you need to be. That's why we gave them to you," Mama says, checking her inventory. She's probably going to make me some more tea. Yuck. I've had enough of that bitter shit to last me a lifetime.

"Especially with the friends you've got running around," Netta says, busy giving my mother work to do. "I heard about Mickey finally confessing that that little baby girl in her stomach is Tre's." I look at Netta across the room, ever amazed at her ability to get information. Tre's sister Brandy comes into the shop whenever she has some money. I guess she found an extra twenty dollars this week and got some things off her chest while in Netta's chair.

"You can't keep bailing your friends out, Jayd," Mama says, taking several branches of dried herbs off the shrine and placing them on the kitchen table.

"But what am I supposed to do? Let them fall apart?" I whine, cuddling up in the warm blanket. The food smells good, but it may have to wait until after I've had a good nap.

"The only thing you can do is work on your influence with each of them. That's it," Netta says, mixing the pancake batter while the turkey bacon sizzles in the other cast-iron skillet. I can't wait to get into our brunch. My mom's cutting fresh strawberries in the sink while Mama sets the table. The spirit room may be small, but it's the perfect holy place for us.

"But I could manipulate Misty's mind through my dreams when she and her evil godmother Esmeralda tried to take over my vision. Why not theirs?"

"Because that little heffa tried to steal your powers, but Nigel and Mickey are different. This is not your battle, Jayd." Mama's right. The best thing I can do is work on perfecting when I can jump into someone's thoughts and how to get out of them.

"Well, what if it is?" I ask, yawning. "Last time Misty went after me, she hurt my friends in the process. This time it looks like she's doing the same thing."

"The best way to get back at Misty is to be strong and healthy. Don't you see, Jayd? The only way Misty has been able to get to you is when you're not feeling well. She has to use your own powers against you in order to take you down because she's not strong enough to do it herself, and neither is Esmeralda." Mama places the last plate on the table and waits for Netta to finish cooking.

"Yeah, but Jayd wasn't asleep when this happened and her

powers lie in her dreams," my mom says, playing detective. I feel her presence in my mind, but as long as I don't think the truth, she can't hear it.

"What you need to do is move your ass back home, but I'm not going to say it again," Mama says, taking a piece of bacon off the plate where Netta has placed it to cool. "But until then you need to rest. And stop eating all that junk at your mama's house, which means you need to provide her with groceries so she doesn't have to spend her hard-earned money buying the cheapest food she can find." My mom sucks her teeth at Mama, but I think she's feeling her. I'm just glad they're talking again.

"Okay, Mama. I'm going to listen to you and take it easy for the next couple days," I say. Mama brings me a small plate of food, forcing me to eat a little before I nod off. It's so good, but will taste even better when I can really enjoy it.

"No, young lady. You're taking weeks off," Mama says, patting my hand. "This isn't a simple cold you can bounce back from, as we have seen from today's episode in church. You need time to fortify yourself, and that will take a while." I knew Mama had something else up her sleeve for me. "These herbs have to be taken in several rounds of doses, and once you finish, your blood will be so strong and your head so cool, nothing will be able to rattle you, not even Misty." That's news to my ears. If it'll make me invincible, I'll try it out. Besides, I can use the mandatory quiet time to completely focus on my studies—friends and their bull not allowed.

It was nice taking a couple weeks off from the drama to focus on myself. Spring break was real chill, with Jeremy keeping me company. Because we were out of school, our study group met every day, all day, leaving our evenings free, and Jeremy and I took full advantage of the off time. We went to the movies, walked along the beach, and ate out every night. It was perfect. I needed to relax in order to be ready for our exams, and I think we are both in a good place to do our best. In order to stay chill once the break was over, I stayed clear of my crew. It's been two weeks since I've talked to Nellie or Mickey outside of class, and I must say, I don't miss them as much as I thought I would. Maybe it's because whenever I've seen them lately, it's been all about them and I'm tired of going along with that conversation. It's time to focus on me, and that starts by passing all my AP exams.

My first test was on Monday. Luckily, it was in economics, and I'm pretty confident I passed that exam and the Spanish one on Wednesday. Today is English. I can't wait to show Mrs. Bennett up. As much as I've been studying, I think I'll get at least a four, if not a five. Passing will be good enough for me at this point, and as the saying goes, revenge is a dish best served cold, and I can't wait to hand it out.

Upon walking into Mrs. Bennett's classroom, I notice Misty standing at the teacher's table sharpening pencils. There's been a student helper in all the exams, usually an office aid like Misty. She looks up from her busy work and smiles at me, pointing to an empty desk in the full room. I wave to Jeremy, who is seated on the other side of the room with most of our crew, including Candace. I can't afford to let anything rattle me this morning, hating hos included.

I take my seat as Mrs. Bennett walks in, closing the door behind her. The force from the door causes the fluorescent light above my desk to flicker like it's about to go out. This can't be a good sign, but I'm staying cool, no matter what happens. I raise my hand to get Mrs. Bennett's attention. She looks annoyed at my very presence, which is no surprise.

"Mrs. Bennett, the light above my head is going out," I say, noticing that my light is the only one having this problem.

"You have all the light you need to see, Jayd," she says, smiling as if this were her master plan all along. Misty passes

out the pencils and test booklets, smiling at the teacher's response. Mrs. Bennett is right. If I can write down a story in
the spirit book in complete darkness in my dream, I can take
this test with the flash of light above my head. I know I can
pass this thing, and doing so will be the sweetest revenge on
both Mrs. Bennett and Misty.

At the end of the grueling three-hour exam, it's finally
time to turn in the papers. Once my booklet is closed, I reach
my hands high above my head and stretch the tension away. I
feel really good about this one. Unlike the first practice test I
took several weeks ago, I knew almost every question, including the essays. All that studying paid off, and so did
Mama's rest regimen. Jeremy looks confident as usual as he
turns in his exam and walks out the door. I get up from my
desk and follow the rest of the students to the teacher's desk
and then off campus for the weekend. I can't wait to celebrate with my man and our newfound AP crew, but first a little payback is due.

"I know I passed," I say to Mrs. Bennett as I turn in my exam.
She looks up at me, her cold blue eyes as fierce as they can
get without the gift of sight present in my lineage. Misty tries
to look at me with her fake aqua eyes, but neither one of them
can shake me today.

"We'll just see about that, Miss Jackson." She takes the
exam booklet and sets it with the rest of the pile. I silently
chant the oriki Netta gave me for my birthday to make sure
my exam gets to where it's supposed to go without any inter-
ference. As I toss my backpack over my left shoulder, my jade
bracelets move down my arm and fall to my wrist, catching
Mrs. Bennett's eye. She looks at the five bangles as if she just
saw a ghost.

"Everything okay?" I ask her, but for the first time ever, the
broad is speechless. Good. Me reclaiming my power is indeed
the sweetest revenge ever. Exacting complete vengeance on

my big-booty nemesis will have to wait until another time. Misty, unfortunately, will never go away. I'll always have to be one step ahead of her to fortify myself against her ill will.

"So how did my girl do?" Jeremy asks, taking my backpack from me and carrying it alongside his.

"I think I did very well. And you?" We walk hand in hand toward the parking lot to our separate cars.

"It's all good," Jeremy says, letting go of my hand and putting his arm around my shoulders. "Now I'm going to surf to celebrate."

"Surf?" I ask. I know he's a beach boy, but that's no way to blow off steam after the heavy load we've been carrying. To each his own, I guess. "But, baby, I thought we might do something fun together."

"Why don't you come to the beach with me and hang out? Or, better yet, you can get in the water with me."

"And mess up my do? No, thank you," I say, touching my smooth ponytail. We get to my ride first, parting ways for now, but I'm sure I'll see him later.

"Okay, Jayd. Then I guess this is good-bye for now," Jeremy says, kissing me before I unlock the doors. "I'll call you tonight when I'm on my way." He walks toward his Mustang parked several spaces down from mine.

"Oh, you just know you're coming over tonight, huh?" We've been practically inseparable since my birthday, and I wouldn't have it any other way.

"Yes, I do. Where else would I be?" Where else, indeed. But now I have nothing to do tonight. Too bad my friends are all in pissy moods. I guess I'll have to settle for a nice, long bath and movies tonight. Before I pull off, Rah calls. We never did talk about what Mickey blurted out at the shower, and I've just been letting him cool off. He must be ready to talk.

"Hey," I say into the phone.

"Hey, Jayd. I want you to know I didn't forget your birthday," he says. "Can you come by tonight and pick up your present?" What he's not saying is that he misses me, and I miss him, too. Maybe we can celebrate my good day together as friends, minus the drama.

"Yeah, and thanks in advance, Rah. I'll see you around nine." We hang up, and I feel good about seeing one of my best friends tonight. But the reunion will have to come after some much deserved me time.

When I pull up to Rah's house, the lights are low, and there are candles lit all over the living room. I can see through the large window that someone's planning a romantic evening in. I guess his mom brings her men home these days. I can hear Sade playing in the background, but I see no one anywhere in sight.

I decide to wait in my car until Rah comes home, but before I can make my way back down the porch toward the driveway, Rah pulls up. Thank God, because the last thing I want to do is witness a love-making scene, especially not where his mom's one of the participants. I'd probably be scarred for life if that happened.

"Hey, girl. I was just about to call you," he says, parking his car in its customary spot and turning off the engine. "Sorry we're late, but I had to pick up my daughter from day care." Rahima waves at me from the backseat, making me smile. I just love that little girl, and I've missed her, too.

"Hey, you two," I say, opening the passenger's door to move the seat up so I can get baby girl out of the back. She almost leaps into my arms as I pick her up and head toward the front door. "I think your mom has company," I say, bending my head toward the romantic scene awaiting us, just in case he wants to go in through the back door.

"Nah, that can't be right. My mom's working a bachelor

party in Palm Springs this weekend," he says, stepping in front of us and opening the screen door. As Rah unlocks the front door to let us in, Sandy appears in the foyer wearing nothing but underwear and high heels—her customary work attire. I stay behind Rah and shield Rahima from the raunchy sight. This bitch is really tripping now.

"Sandy, what the hell is wrong with you? Go put on some clothes!" Rah yells as he walks to the couch, grabs a throw off the back of it, and tosses it at his slutty houseguest. Sandy looks past him and at me, foaming at the mouth like a pit bull infested with rabies. I guess I ruined her romantic evening. This girl is too much, and Rah needs to put her ass out sooner than later before she causes him any more trouble. If my dream about Sandy and Rahima in a near-fatal collision due to Sandy's negligence is any indication of what's to come in the future, Rah better get out while he still can.

"What is she doing here? Don't you ever go home?" Sandy asks, covering herself, but the miniature blanket is too small to cover all she's packing, and she knows it, too.

"Don't you?" I ask, returning the inquiry. She reaches for Rahima on my hip, who pulls away from her mother. At least Rahima's got good taste and sense, too. I smile at Sandy, who looks more pissed than hurt by her daughter's action. Following Rah's lead, I leave Sandy to clean up her mess and head to the back where the studio is housed. If it weren't for Rah's music, he'd have no escape from his ever-dramatic life.

"She's not your baby, and he's not your man!" Sandy yells after us. If it weren't for that damn ankle bracelet she's attached to, I'm sure Rah would have thrown her out for that little stunt. Now completely hot, Rah turns the music up loud and tries to block out Sandy's irrational behavior. I would say "I told you so" about letting Sandy serve out her house arrest here, but now's not the time. The girl's crazy, just like my mom said, and there's no saving the insane. Sandy has to want to change, and from the looks of her moves so far, it seems she doesn't care to for her or her daughter's sake.

"Daddy," Rahima says, reaching her arms out toward her father, but he can't hear her through Marvin Gaye's sad voice blaring through the speakers. I know he wants to holler, just like the song says, but he can't. And as his friend, I want to scream for him.

"Give me the keys," Sandy says, interrupting our healing session. "I'm taking my baby out of here." Pushing me back, she snatches Rahima out of my arms and walks toward the back door that leads outside.

"You can't go anywhere, and even if you could, you know can't drive my car again, ever, or take my baby wherever you go." Sandy stares at Rahima, who leaps into her daddy's arms as soon as she gets the chance. Rah's not the type to hit a woman, but I'd understand if he wanted to shake the shit out of Sandy. I would.

"You're an ass, you know that?" Sandy says, punching Rah in the arm hard. Even though she's slightly shorter than him, she's stacked and outweighs him by a good thirty or so pounds. I stand by the door leading into the kitchen and watch the tragic scene unfold. I would go rescue Rahima, but I'm not moving. And I know Rah won't let anything happen to his little girl. Too bad he has to protect her from her own mother. That's why I'm not the one to rush into sex, no matter how good they say it feels.

"Don't hit me again, Sandy. I'm not playing with you." The tightness in Rah's already clenched jaw heightens as the tension in the room rises. Rahima lies against her father's chest, looking like she's ready for her bath and bedtime story. Rah glances at me, remembering there's a witness, and relaxes his stance, and I'm glad for it, although I do understand the temptation to knock her mean ass out, once and for all. I don't care how much Sandy weighs, Rah's a strong man and can take her with one blow, but I know he'd never bring himself to that place.

"What are you going to do about it, punk? You'd never hit a girl," she taunts, slapping him hard on the cheek. The loud sound of the hit shocks both me and Rah, who loosens his grasp on Rahima at the impact. Sandy snatches Rahima away from Rah, who looks mad enough to hit the wall. Rahima starts to cry again as we all wait for the next move.

"Tomorrow morning you need to be out of my house, Sandy. Go call your parole officer and pack your shit."

"I'd better go," I say, voluntarily excusing myself from the situation. Mama already told me about fighting my friends' battles, and this is definitely not what I had in mind tonight. I guess I'll be celebrating by myself after all.

"But your gift," Rah says, torn between arguing with Sandy and walking me out.

"I'll get it next time, really." I open the front door and leave Rah's home for the evening, maybe for good. My friends seem addicted to drama, and I let that go when Mama gave me my last bout of sweet herbs to heal me. Because of her magic I can't stomach the bull anymore. I hope Rah's not a casualty of my newfound attitude, but if he is, that's a price I'm willing to pay to save myself.

Epilogue

It's a typical quiet Sunday afternoon at Mama's house. I'm glad she was in the mood to cook today because I can use a home-cooked meal. My mom's paying for some of my groceries, but nothing compares to what my grandmother can whip up. Mama covers the pot of greens and lowers the fire underneath to let them simmer. The house stinks something good, as my mom would say. Even if greens don't give off the best scent, their smell still makes my mouth water.

"Jayd, go ahead and start the cornbread for me, please." I take the carton of eggs and milk out of the refrigerator before retrieving the rest of the ingredients from the cupboard. You can't eat greens without a sweet batch of Mama's buttermilk cornbread. It's just not natural. I came over after work so Mama could see for herself that I'm doing just fine, even after last night's encounter with Rah and Sandy. Like Mickey, that girl is hell-bent on disaster.

"Do you want me to season the chicken when I'm done?" I ask, taking out the poultry spices, too.

"You can." Mama's been in a good mood lately. I guess the sweet-words spell is still in full effect. She and my mom have even started laughing more when they're on the phone. I'm happy it all worked out for the best, even if it was a difficult journey. They were also excited about me feeling like I did well on my exams. I think Mama was more excited about me being able to return to my normal work hours at the shop and possibly come back home, but I'm not ready for that. I like living at my mom's, and not just because Jeremy has practically moved in. I also like having the freedom to relax and the peace and quiet to do it right. Last night I stayed in the bathtub for over an hour. My skin was wrinkled, and the water heater ran out of hot water because I refilled the tub so many times, but no one was rushing me. This type of freedom is priceless, and, like my mother's sight, I'm not giving it up anytime soon. I feel stronger than ever before, and I have a good feeling that it's only going to get nicer from here. I may have to fight to maintain my independence, but it's nothing I can't handle.

Drama High, Volume 11:

COLD AS ICE

L. Divine

ABOUT THIS GUIDE

The following questions are intended to
enhance your group's reading of
DRAMA HIGH: COLD AS ICE
by L. Divine.

DISCUSSION QUESTIONS

1. Do you think Jayd is working too hard in school and doing hair? Should she give up on being a straight-A student, working after school, or a little of both?
2. Mrs. Bennett seems to always have it out for Jayd. How would you recommend Jayd go about having a teacher reprimanded for her personal vendetta against a student?
3. Do you think Jayd should take care of Misty, once and for all, if possible? How so?
4. Do you know of homemade remedies for healing a cold? If so, what are they, and do they work?
5. Does Jeremy spoil Jayd too much? Do you think Jayd is taking advantage of being with a rich white boy? Explain.
6. Do you think Nigel's mom should be nicer to Mickey or continue to give her the cold shoulder? Why or why not?
7. Do you get nervous speaking in front of crowds? How do you handle it?
8. Do you think Jayd should be honest and tell Mama about her newfound powers? Do you think she should tell her mom? Why or why not?

9. Now that Jayd has found a new study group to chill with, should she give up on Nellie and Mickey for good?

10. Is it realistic for Jayd to remain a virgin in a relationship that is as close as her and Jeremy's? Why or why not?

11. Have you ever taken revenge on someone who did you wrong? If so, how? How did it make you feel afterward?

12. Do you think Jayd made the right decision by leaving Mama's house and moving into her mom's apartment? Explain.

13. Do you enjoy challenging classes? Why or why not?

14. Should Jayd finally tell Chance that he's adopted, especially now that his mother found out that Jayd knows the truth?

Jaydism #3

Steam baths work wonders for the body, skin, and soul. Soak in a hot tub (not too hot!) for at least twenty minutes, allowing the steam to work its magic. You'll feel clean and refreshed afterward.

Stay tuned for the next book in
the DRAMA HIGH series,
PUSHIN'

Until then, satisfy your DRAMA HIGH craving
with the following excerpt from the next
exciting installment

ENJOY!

Prologue

Ever since I left Rah's house Friday evening, he's been blowing my cell up, and I just don't have the energy to deal with his bull. Mama and I have been cooking all afternoon, providing me with the perfect distraction. After eating a slamming dinner of chicken, rice, greens, and cornbread, a sistah is stuffed. All I really want to do is pass out on my mom's couch and watch television for the rest of the night, but I doubt Mama's letting me go any time soon. Since moving out a few weeks ago, Mama's made it her personal mission to keep me here as long as she possibly can on my now regular Sunday visits. And as long as I can get a good meal out of it, I won't protest too much, even if the itis is setting in.

"Jayd, hand me that white fabric on the table, please," Mama says from where she's seated on the floor across from the kitchen table. I stack the last of the clean dishes on the rack, dry my hands off on one of the yellow kitchen towels hanging from the cabinet above the sink, and hand her the stack of folded cloth.

"Thank you," Mama says, taking the cotton fabric and placing it in one of several large bags sitting on the bamboo mat around her. Mama's in full initiation mode, and with the weather officially warming up, it's just the beginning of her busy season as the head priestess in charge. All the spiritual houses in Los Angeles County call on Mama's expertise, and I get to tag along as her assistant, even when I don't especially feel like it. I sit down in one of the chairs at the table and fan my face with my hand. It's a warm evening, and with the way we threw down, the spirit room is still hot from the stove being on all day.

"Well, I guess I'd better get ready for the bembé," I say, looking up at the clock on the wall. We've been back here for hours, eating, talking, laughing. The sweet spell I put on Mama and my mom at Daddy's church on Easter a few weeks ago has worked its magic, and I couldn't have asked for a better outcome. I missed the last spiritual party celebrating the end of an initiation because of Misty's trifling ass. I'm not initiated yet, and can't participate in all the ins and outs of the rituals, but, as Mama's apprentice, I help in every other way. I was secretly hoping I'd start my cycle so I wouldn't have to help tonight, but no such luck. Any other time I'd be bleeding all over the place, but it's late this month. I wanted to take the time to catch up on my spirit work, focusing on my latest acquisition. Possessing my mom's gift of sight is a trip, and I want to learn more about controlling it. Keeping my newfound powers a secret has been no easy task, but so far, so good.

"I think your ashe is still too vulnerable to attend any spiritual festivities tonight, but there will be another bembé soon," Mama says, unknowingly granting my silent wish. She opens the spirit book sitting next to her and directs me to sit across from her on the mat. "Read that section and take a honey bath when you get . . . home," she says, stuttering on her last word. Tears cloud Mama's jade eyes and fall to the page, permanently smudging the ancient black ink.

"Oh, Mama," I say, reaching across the mat to hug my grandmother. I hate it when she cries. "I miss you, too." And I do. I also miss Daddy, Jay, and my crazy uncle Bryan. It's the rest of the fools up in the house I'm glad to be rid of.

"Why do I lose all my girls?" Mama asks, holding me tightly. The faint scent of garlic and rosemary drifts upward from her apron, tickling my nose. Both of her daughters moved out the first chance they got, and so did I. I can't speak for Jay's mama or mine, but Mama has to realize how hard it is being the only young woman in a house full of men.

"It's not you. But living with all these dudes is a bit much," I say, holding on to Mama for one more second before letting go. Mama looks into my eyes and I into hers, trying to use my mom's cooling gifts on her mind, but it's still no use. Mama's too powerful for my tricks.

"I'd better get dressed before Netta gets here," Mama says, rising from the floor and making her way to the door. It's hard for Mama to understand why everyone can't be as strong as she is, just like I can't understand for the life of me why she chooses to stay with a husband who cheats on her and with trifling sons who don't respect her house.

"Maybe you and I can get a place of our own," I say. Mama smiles and kisses me on the cheek.

"You are so sweet. And so young," she says, taking three of the bags and directing me to claim the other three from the mat. I follow her out of the spirit room and into the main house. It's still too early in the evening for my uncles to come home, and Daddy's probably having dinner at the church. Bryan and Jay are watching television in the living room and look less than enthusiastic to see us walk through the kitchen door. We set the bags down on the dining room table, checking to make sure we've got everything.

"Have fun, Mama, and tell Netta I said hi," I say, kissing her on the cheek. Jay and Bryan look up at me and wave before returning their attention to the *Bernie Mac* rerun on the screen.

"Will do, baby, and see you tomorrow afternoon at work," Mama says, quickly hugging me before heading to her room to get dressed for the party. I'm sure she'll look brilliant in her all-white clothing, as always. "And don't forget your spirit work, Jayd!" Mama yells from her room. Little does she know, that's all I can think about. I'm looking forward to looking through the spirit book for more information on my mom's powers and clues as to how I can keep them. I have to be careful not to tip Mama or my mom off, or my new sight will be gone before I can master it, and I'm not ready for that yet. I want to be as dope as Mama is with her shit and as bad as my mom was when she had complete control of her mind-altering powers. And to get that flyy, I've got a lot of work to do, starting right now.

~ 1 ~
Say What?

*"You can be as good as the best of them /
but as bad as the worst /
so don't test me.
You better move over."*

—Notorious B.I.G.

Making my way out of the kitchen and through the back-yard, I notice Lexi following me to the backhouse. She takes her guardian job way too seriously, if you ask me. I open the screen door and lock it behind me, lest anyone decides to surprise me back here, which I doubt. The boys rarely go any farther than the garage attached to the front of the small house. They don't know exactly what we do back here, nor do they want to.

"Finally, some alone time in the spirit room," I say to Lexi, who looks uninterested in my enthusiasm. I wish I could read her mind, but, unfortunately, my newfound sight doesn't work on dogs. I have a couple hours before Jeremy meets me back at my mom's, and I want to get as much work done as I can. Before I can get into my studying, my phone vibrates with another call from Rah. Now what?

"Hey, girl," Rah says groggily through my cell. When I left his house Friday night, he and Sandy were still going hard. I've got too much work to do today to be his shoulder, and I need to make this call quick if I want to take full advantage of my alone time.

"What's up, Rah? I'm at Mama's," I say while turning from the page that Mama left open for me to study, instead searching for my own shit. I'll take the bath as prescribed and do some of my assignment, but tonight is all about me.

"Can you come over on your way home? I have a little something for you I meant to give you Friday." He can't be serious. There's no way in hell I'm stepping back into his house as long as Sandy's Amazonian ass is there. "Sandy's gone to her grandparents' house for the weekend." Rah's no mind reader, but he hit that one on the head. I thought he told her to move out, but I don't have time to get the full story.

"It'll have to be quick because I already have plans for the evening," I say, glancing at the wall clock and then down at the work in front of me. It's going to take me at least a couple hours to finish up here, and I told Jeremy I'd be back in Inglewood by nine, which means I'll have to leave here and get to Rah's by eight to make it back to my mom's on time.

"Cool. See you later," Rah says. I hang up my cell and focus on the task at hand. I don't know why I keep bending to Rah's will, but I'm getting stronger in more ways than one. Besides, a gift is a gift, and who am I to say no? A true friend forgives, and I have no problem with that; as long as Rah doesn't mistake my kindness for weakness—again—it's all good.

It was nice working alone on my spirit work, and it was just the peace I needed to get my mind right for the week ahead. I'm working extra hard to get Mama the stove she so deserves for Mother's Day and to make up for all the work I missed studying for my Advanced Placement exams last week. Luckily, summer's around the corner, and with my main job at Netta's and my side hustle doing hair at my mom's place, my cheddar should be well stacked in a few months.

I've been at Rah's house for all of ten minutes, and already his cell phone is working my nerves. He's been in his room talking since I got here, and I'm ready to go. If I leave now, I could take a shower and relax before Jeremy arrives, not that he cares much how I look these days. We just like being together, morning breath and all.

"Rah, I'm out!" I shout from where I'm seated in the living room and head toward the front door.

"Oh no, you don't," he says, jogging into the foyer with a small gold box in hand. He hangs up his cell and hands me my gift. Finally. My birthday was six weeks ago, but just because it's late doesn't mean I won't accept it. I look up at my boy and smile, opening the box.

"Oh, Rah, it's beautiful," I say, pulling out the gold ankh charm hanging from a shiny gold chain. He's never bought me something so extravagant before. This must've set him back at least a bill or two. With my gold "Lady J" bangle from Jeremy, I'm starting myself a nice little collection of boyfriend jewelry. Mickey's the one with the jewelry box full of shiny things from all her conquests, but my two pieces are nothing to laugh at either.

"I know your birthday passed, and I acted like a jackass, but I wanted to still give you your gift," he says, taking the heavy necklace from my hands and walking behind me. "Let me help you put it on." I move my hair from my left shoulder to my right and hold it up slightly so he can see what he's doing. After securing the cold metal around my neck, he bends down and kisses me gently. He knows my neck is extra sensitive, especially in the groove between my ear and shoulder on either side.

"Rah, I've got to go," I say, trying to resist his soft lips, but he ignores my request and keeps kissing, now almost sucking my skin. If he doesn't stop soon, I'm going to have a hickey on my neck the size of Long Beach to explain to Mama and everyone else with eyes, including Jeremy.

"Do you really want me to stop?" Rah asks, moving his

hips from side to side and me right along with him. Damn, he feels good—too good. His phone vibrates in his jeans pocket, and just in time, too. I almost got caught up in the rapture with this brotha, and that is the wrong direction to go in.

"I've got to get this. Don't go anywhere," Rah says, stepping into the living room. I should really get going, but before I can escape, I hear something in the back. As Rah continues his conversation, Sandy walks through the studio door that connects to the kitchen; she has Rahima on her hip. Why didn't she come in through the front door like she normally would?

"I saw you two making out through the window," Sandy says—no hi, hello, or nothing. Where are her manners? "Are you going to stand there and tell me you haven't given up the panties yet?" she asks, throwing her cell phone down on the counter. Rahima looks freighted but stays glued to her mother, who has little regard that her daughter is still in the room.

"Well, hello to you, too," I say, waving at my girl, who waves back in her cute two-year-old way. It looks more like snatching than waving, but I'll take what I can get.

"Please, Jayd, y'all can cut the act." She takes a pot out of the cabinet under the stove and walks over to the sink, filling it with water like she's about to cook, but we both know that's not what she's doing.

"Say what?" I ask, completely offended by her accusation, and so is Rah, who finally walks into the kitchen to deal with his irrational baby-mama. This is my cue to roll.

"Sandy, you're talking like you're crazy. Did you take your meds today?" Rah asks, but there's nothing funny about Sandy's behavior.

"Don't play with me, fool. I know what I saw." Sandy's eyes are more evil than usual. I hope she's not planning to cook grits, because I do not want to witness an Al Green moment. Besides, she has no right reacting about Rah and me doing anything together, even if she's way off. Why is she the only one who doesn't see that?

Because she's right to some degree, my mom says, reasoning for the wrong side.

Mom, not now. Please. I can't tell, but I think my mom's laughing at my plea to get her out of my mind. Like I have any control over that. Maybe I can work on that part of my vision, too.

"Sandy, you need to relax. We already established this last time you tried to pull this shit. You're not my wife, and I don't have to answer to you. We're not a family, Sandy," Rah says. His phone rings again, and he goes back into the living room to answer it. Sandy looks at me like she wants to slit my throat with one of the knives by the stove. If I could fly over there, I'd move them out of her reach, but no such luck.

"I've got to make a run real quick," he says, coming back into the foyer where I'm posted. "Jayd, you want to come with me?"

"All right," I agree. Anywhere is better than being here with Sandy, and I want to make it clear to Rah that he can't kiss me like that anymore. Jeremy and I are definitely one-on-one these days, and he needs to respect that. Rah puts his keys on the counter out of habit, and Sandy snatches them up, holding them hostage.

"Y'all ain't going nowhere," she says, throwing the keys out of the open kitchen window. If Rah's mom kept up with the house, there would be a screen there preventing Sandy's erratic behavior.

"Sandy, what the hell did you do that for?" Rah yells at a smiling Sandy. Rahima leaps from her mother's arms and runs to her father, who picks her up, holding her tight.

"I've got to go," I say, opening the door behind me and heading away from the ugly scene. I can holla at Rah later. He puts Rahima down and heads out the front door behind me.

I wave good-bye to Rahima, who's now back in her mother's arms. Poor baby. She doesn't know which way to go, and I feel her. Sandy runs out of the kitchen and through the back door. Rah and I stare at each other as we hear his car door slam and the engine start.

"Bye, bitches!" she yells, pulling away from the curb and speeding down the street. She must've found another spare key. I thought he learned his lesson the last time she stole his grandfather's car, but I guess not. If my dream about her driving fast was any indication of what's ahead, I need to warn Rah.

"We have to stop her," I say to him, but Rah just looks after his red car speeding down the street, completely dazed. "Come on." I run over to my mom's car parked in the driveway, but he doesn't move.

"Man, I'm done chasing that trick. Let her parole officer catch her," Rah says, not realizing how serious the situation is. He looks down at his ringing cell and silences it for the moment. What the hell?

"Rah, she's out of control, with your daughter in the back-seat. Don't you care about Rahima's well-being?" I open the car door and get in, starting the engine. If we leave now, we may be able to catch Sandy at the light.

"That's what I'm saying," he says, sending a text to God only knows who. "When she gets busted for being out past her curfew, she'll be in violation of her parole and back in jail, and I'll have Rahima once and for all. Besides, I've got something to handle real quick. Can you drive, baby?" What the hell did this fool just say to me? And is Rah seriously putting his hustle over his daughter's safety in the hopes that Sandy will get busted? Really?

"Rah, I'm telling you Sandy driving with Rahima is a bad idea. I had a dream about her getting into an accident where they both get seriously hurt." Rah gets into the passenger's seat and looks at me, stroking my cheek with his left hand.

"Jayd, Rahima's in the car with her mother every day, and nothing that bad has ever happened. Maybe your dream meant something else," he says, patronizing me. Rah's never going to take me seriously when it comes to what's best for Rahima, and I see that clearly now. "Now, can we go, please? That girl's already got me running late."

"Find another way to get there. I'm going home," I say, pushing Rah out of my mom's ride and shutting the door behind him. I already know where this road leads, and I refuse to go down it with him anymore. I've been way too nice about this entire situation, and however their mess ends, I want no part of it.

START YOUR OWN BOOK CLUB

Courtesy of the DRAMA HIGH series

ABOUT THIS GUIDE

The following is intended to help you get
the book club you've always wanted
up and running!
Enjoy!

Start Your Own Book Club

A Book Club is not only a great way to make friends, but it is also a fun and safe environment for you to express your views and opinions on everything from fashion to teen pregnancy. A Teen Book Club can also become a forum or venue to air grievances and plan remedies for problems.

The People

To start, all you need is yourself and at least one other person. There's no criteria for who this person or persons should be other than their having a desire to read and a commitment to discuss things during a certain time frame.

The Rules

Just as in Jayd's life, sometimes even Book Club discussions can be filled with much drama. People tend to disagree with each other, cut each other off when speaking, and take criticism personally. So, there should be some ground rules:

1. Do not attack people for their ideas or opinions.
2. When you disagree with a Book Club member on a point, disagree respectfully. This means that you do not denigrate other people or their ideas, i.e., no name-calling or saying, "That's stupid!" Instead, say, "I can respect your position; however, I feel differently."
3. Back up your opinions with concrete evidence, either from the book in question or life in general.
4. Allow everyone a turn to comment.
5. Do not cut a member off when the person is speaking. Respectfully wait your turn.
6. Critique only the idea. Do not criticize the person.

7. Every member must agree to and abide by the ground rules.

Feel free to add any other ground rules you think might be necessary.

The Meeting Place

Once you've decided on members, and agreed to the ground rules, you should decide on a place to meet. This could be the local library, the school library, your favorite restaurant, a bookstore, or a member's home. Remember, though, if you decide to hold your sessions at a member's home, the location should rotate to another member's home for the next session. It's also polite for guests to bring treats when attending a Book Club meeting at a member's home. If you choose to hold your meetings in a public place, always remember to ask the permission of the librarian or store manager. If you decide to hold your meetings in a local bookstore, ask the manager to post a flyer in the window announcing the Book Club to attract more members if you so desire.

Timing Is Everything

Teenagers of today are all much busier than teenagers of the past. You're probably thinking, "Between chorus rehearsals, the Drama Club, and oh yeah, my job, when will I ever have time to read another book that doesn't feature Romeo and Juliet!" Well, there's always time, if it's time well-planned and time planned ahead. You and your Book Club can decide to meet as often or as little as is appropriate for your bustling schedules. *Once a month* is a favorite option. *Sleepover Book Club* meetings—if you're open to excluding one gender—is also a favorite option. And in this day of high-tech, savvy teens, *Internet Discussion Groups* are also an appealing option. Just choose what's right for you!

Well, you've got the people, the ground rules, the place, and the time. All you need now is a book!

The Book

Choosing a book is the most fun. COLD AS ICE is of course an excellent choice, and since it's part of a series, you won't soon run out of books to read and discuss. Your Book Club can also have comparative discussions as you compare the first book, THE FIGHT, to the second, SECOND CHANCE, and so on.

But depending upon your reading appetite, you may want to veer outside of the Drama High series. That's okay. There are plenty of options, many of which you will be able to find under the Dafina Books for Young Readers Program in the coming months.

But don't be afraid to mix it up. Nonfiction is just as good as fiction and a fun way to learn about from where we came without just using a history textbook. Science fiction and fantasy can be fun, too!

And always, always research the author. You might find that the author has a Web site where you can post your Book Club's questions or comments. The author may even have an e-mail address available so you can correspond directly. Authors might also sit in on your Book Club meetings, either in person, or on the phone, and this can be a fun way to discuss the book as well!

The Discussion

Every good Book Club discussion starts with questions. COLD AS ICE, as does every book in the Drama High series, comes with a Reading Group Guide for your convenience, though of course, it's fine to make up your own. Here are some sample questions to get started:

1. What's this book all about anyway?
2. Who are the characters? Do we like them? Do they remind us of real people?
3. Was the story interesting? Were real issues that are of concern to you examined?
4. Were there details that didn't quite work for you or ring true?
5. Did the author create a believable environment—one that you could visualize?
6. Was the ending satisfying?
7. Would you read another book from this author?

Record Keeper

It's generally a good idea to have someone keep track of the books you read. Often libraries and schools will hold reading drives where you're rewarded for having read a certain number of books in a certain time period. Perhaps a pizza party awaits!

Get Your Teachers and Parents Involved

Teachers and parents love it when kids get together and read. So involve your teachers and parents. Your Book Club may read a particular book whereby it would help to have an adult's perspective as part of the discussion. Teachers may also be able to include what you're doing as a Book Club in the classroom curriculum. That way, books you love to read, such as the Drama High ones, can find a place in your classroom alongside the books you don't love to read so much.

Resources

To find some new favorite writers, check out the following resources. Happy reading!

Young Adult Library Services Association
http://www.ala.org/ala/yalsa/yalsa.htm

Carnegie Library of Pittsburgh
Hip-Hop!
Teen Rap Titles
http://www.carnegielibrary.org/teens/read/booklists/teen rap.html

TeensPoint.org
What Teens Are Reading
http://www.teenspoint.org/reading_matters/book_list.asp? sort=5&list=274

Teenreads.com
http://www.teenreads.com

Sacramento Public Library
Fantasy Reading for Kids
http://www.saclibrary.org/teens/fantasy.html

Book Divas
http://www.bookdivas.com

Meg Cabot Book Club
http://www.megcabotbookclub.com

GREAT BOOKS, GREAT SAVINGS!

When You Visit Our Website:
www.kensingtonbooks.com

You Can Save Money Off The Retail Price
Of Any Book You Purchase!

- **All Your Favorite Kensington Authors**
- **New Releases & Timeless Classics**
- **Overnight Shipping Available**
- **eBooks Available For Many Titles**
- **All Major Credit Cards Accepted**

Visit Us Today To Start Saving!
www.kensingtonbooks.com